Tainted Love

"What's done in the dark…"

J.L.Crayton

Tainted Love

Copyright © 2015

Disclaimer

Dedication

This book is dedicated to the New Generation. Change the way you think. Positive people and positive environments will always make you elevate your way of thinking. Remember your actions have consequences.

Perhaps you're curious as to the title of my story. Well, this runs deep. I was inundated with many questions as I contemplated writing this story. Suffice it to say, I listened to others, got some input here and there, and I also explored various topics; and interestingly enough, the word, 'tainted' was etched in my thoughts. It lingered... then, I double-checked its definitions...

Tainted (taint, tainting, taints): (1) A trace of something bad, offensive, or harmful. A trace of infection, contamination, or the like. (2) To affect or associate with something undesirable or reprehensible. (3) To expose to an infectious agent, toxin, or undesirable substance.

Love: (1) An intense feeling of deep affection, romantic or sexual attachment to someone. (2) A profound, tender, passionate affection for another person.

These definitions best describe the situation that young Tiana was grappling with as a result of the not-too-favorable decisions she made, and the crowd she ultimately chose to hang with. Remember, there are consequences for our actions; some are harsh, while others are not too severe. That, however, doesn't necessarily signal an end of existence.

Here's hoping that by sharing this story, it will bring redemption...and restore hope to someone who has seemingly surrendered the will to go on. Sometimes in life, we just have to look at things from a different perspective, upside down perhaps, sideways, too and take comfort in God's divine providence that when we think all is lost, (God) sends angels to protect, guide, heal and restore.

He also uses us as an inspiration to others; not to save the world, but to endeavor to reach even one individual at a time. Furthermore, my experiences have only fortified my will to face life's challenges and to become a beacon of hope to those who are hurting. Having been given the opportunity to become a voice for a special group of children, this experience has further helped me to inwardly reflect and have a deeper understanding of my calling.

I take comfort in knowing that God has never relinquished His love for us even when we fail Him. Therefore, giving up should never be an option. So, lest we forget, it's never over until God says it's over.

I'm delighted at the prospects of being that unseen voice and sharing my experiences of just how I became the person God has called me to be.

Now let's get started....

Chapter 1

"Good Morning. My name is Ms. Willis, Jay Willis. I have a 9:00a.m.session with Dr. Maxwell."

"Ok, please sign in and have a seat. I'll let the doctor know you're here," the receptionist assured.

"Thank you," I replied.

"Ms. Willis!"

"Yes!"

"Please follow me."

I sprang from my chair and followed her petite frame. "Man, what have I gotten myself into?" I mumbled to myself. Do I really want to do this? Well, I'm here now, so it's too late; I can't back down. I need this. I need to feel better about this whole ordeal, or at least try to make sense of it. And if this is where it begins, then, so be it.

"Hello, I'm Dr. Maxwell," the short, stocky, bald physician interrupted my thoughts. "Have a seat. I heard you really wanted to see me."

"Not really, but someone thought it would be a good idea for me to talk with you to help relieve me of all this stress that I'm going through, and all the suppressed anger I have."

"Stress and anger. Hmm, well, what's wrong?"

"Don't you know?"

"I kind of know bits and pieces but I need to hear it in its entirety directly from you. It's just you and me, so go ahead; talk to me, Ms. Willis. What seems to be bothering you?"

With a dubious mindset, I immediately quipped, "Doc, I don't think you have that kind of time."

"Why would you say that?" he queried with a twitch of the forehead.

"Because it's a lot. It's a mighty long story, Doc. You have to have the time to listen."

"Well, we have an hour."

My heart was racing a bit. "An hour? Man….I might as well head for the door, because an hour isn't enough time. Aaagh, let me see… What are your rates again?"

"Why do you ask? My fee for first time visits is seventy five dollars an hour. So, let's make this hour count."

(Pulling a stack of money from my purse, I said) "How about you bill me."

"Ma'am, wait, well, I tell you what….how about I cancel the rest of my morning so we can spend some time together, talking. Would that be better?"

"Cool," I interjected.

"Now, where do I begin? Well….I'll never forget that day….You see, it was a Saturday morning. It was early, a kind of morning where you routinely hop out of bed late and just lounge around with nothing much to do, it was the day before Father's Day. My alarm clock read 7:12a.m. I remember it like it was yesterday. The phone rang and abruptly awoke me out of a deep sleep, the kind of sleep where you're in Utopia, dreaming and fantasizing about the perfect world and perfect happenings. But, somehow I wasn't completely awake. I heard my mother's piercing screams coming from her bedroom. "Noooo, oh God, no!" she screamed frantically. My basic reflexes summoned immediate action, and I tried springing from the bed. But my body was numb and my thoughts were blurred. I was temporarily immobilized. I knew that something terrible had happened. The bed must have gripped my feet because I spent the remaining fifteen minutes glued beneath the blanket, confused. It felt like I was in the middle of a bad dream, so I smothered my head with the pillow and made a desperate attempt at falling back to sleep.

A few minutes later, I heard my brother scurrying up the hallway crying. He dashed into my room and tapped me on my foot.

"Jay, wake up, wake up Jay!" He wailed desperately.

"What! what! I'm up! I'm up! What's wrong? What happened? Why are you crying?" I questioned, stuttering.

He took a deep breath and began to utter the words incoherently, "TIANA, it's Tiana, she's d-d-dead!"

Nothing was making any sense to me. A bit disoriented, I managed to read his trembling lips as he yelled, "Did you hear me? TIANA'S DEAD!" Something ripped through my heart and I began to shake. I couldn't come to grips with the words that had just come out of his mouth. All I know is that the girl I called my homie, my ride-or-die, my best friend, my niece, was gone! Tiana was gone. I didn't understand why. But this was the beginning of my tragic story.

My name is Jay, but everybody calls me Doll. Lately I've been having some strange feelings about this concept called life. A simple abstraction that can be confusing and equally intriguing. You see, growing up in beautiful Orlando is not always about this place being the ideal tourist paradise with attractive fantasy theme parks. Not all dreams come true in this 'magical kingdom' as the media portrays. There are no fairies floating around with magical wands to transform dreams into reality…The euphoric feeling you experience here lasts only a few days, perhaps fleeting hours; but, in time, you are whisked back into reality...the reality of abject poverty and death; the daily struggles that normal people face is real here. People are suffering, hurting, yearning to experience the true meaning of happiness. These harsh streets will teach you. There is never a day where life's lessons are not being taught, deliberately or not; somewhere someone is tasting the harsh realities of life. Some may grasp it quicker than others, while others move at their own pace. But the lesson that I've learned is dealing with trust.

Learning that you need not trust any man/woman's words. Their actions will always speak louder than their words. And someone will either betray you or let you down in one way or another. Life will teach you that there will be disappointments; no exceptions. You just have to learn to accept things and people for who and what they are. We can discriminate the things that are worth accepting and those that are not. By doing so, we save ourselves a wealth of heartaches that will unquestionably arise when we make the wrong choices. "Why do you feel like that, Ms. Willis?" the doctor inquired curiously.

"If you only knew," I mumbled awkwardly.

"Well, ummm, that's why I'm here. Let's talk about it."

"It's a lot; as a matter of fact, I thought you were already aware of my situation. I thought you knew."

"Knew what?" he questioned.

"The reason I'm here."

"Ms. Willis, again, I was told bits and pieces, but you are supposed to tell me what's wrong. Now, talk to me. What's wrong?"

"Take a wild guess." I urged him.

"Ms. Willis, I don't know."

"Please, Call me Jay, and are you serious? I thought my friend told you."

"Look, Ms. Willis, I mean, Jay; sorry, but, you're wasting my time. If you're not going to talk about what's eating at you, then, you leave me with no option but to end this session. Remember we don't have all day. Now, for the last time, are you going to talk or not?" he demanded calmly but firmly.

"Okay, I'm sorry!' I apologized embarrassingly.

"I'm sorry for my unnecessary babbling; I'm just trying to find the correct words to say. But I'm ready now, so, here it goes…

The reason I said I have an issue with trusting is because of my niece, Tiana. You see, ever since Tiana died, I felt like a part of me died, too. A piece of my heart was ripped from my chest when I got that tragic news. I was angry, I wanted revenge, and I was hurting really badly. I just couldn't and still cannot understand why. Why, Tiana….Why?"

"Listen, Jay, I know you're hurting but I have a question: Why has trusting someone been so hard since Tiana died?"

I questioned myself, dazed and confused. "I never expected someone so close to meet this terrible fate. This loss meant everything to me. I'll never come to grips with such an unspeakable tragedy," I lamented.

"I can hear it in your voice that it means a lot to you, the doctor interrupted.

"Sorry, continue…"

"Well, as I was saying, my family was betrayed in a major way. You know how you see or hear things on TV or you hear about things that people go through? But, it never bothers you because it has absolutely nothing to do with you; or, as they say, it doesn't affect you until it hits home. Well, this particular situation did hit home, my home, both literally and figuratively.

Tiana was in love, and when you're in love, there's the tendency to become blind to a lot of things, especially when it comes to your significant other. It's not deliberately, but sometimes you just fail to pay attention to the signs; nothing matters because you feel that your love can do no wrong. You see Doc, I thought...well, Tiana thought, oh hell, we all thought that her man could do no wrong. He was always the perfect gentleman in our circle of friends or in public; but unfortunately, behind closed doors, it was a different story. Man, I just can't accept that she's not here; I will never accept that she's gone. There's not a day that goes by that I don't think about her. She was more than just my niece, she was my friend. We've had our ups and downs, and even stopped speaking for a few years. But through it all, we were family...we are family. No matter what, we will always be family. And I was there when she needed me most. Through all the hurt and pain, I was her voice. When others turned their backs on her, I was her voice. I will say it in the present tense.....I am her voice. I come from a huge family. My grandmother had twelve children in whom she instilled the value of life and the importance of family values. And not surprisingly, my mother did the same. You see, I grew up in a household with both parents. It was short-lived, however, because that two-parent household became a one parent shortly after I started middle school. My mom became a single parent of three girls and eight boys. Yes, you heard me right... eleven kids in one house. My mother was a hardworking woman, and still is. She worked all the time, making sure that we had shelter over our heads, food on the table and clothes on our backs. She always tried her best to stay involved in all our activities no matter what. We were always busy with school, sports and church, and mom was just as busy, too. It was school practice and church, or, school practice and chores.

We had our daily individual routine down pat. Man, we never even needed a babysitter to stay with us at nights. And you can imagine the things that went on while momma was at work. Kids will be kids and teens will be teens…well, you catch my drift. And I'm reminded of that age-old adage: what you do in the dark will come to light eventually. Well, it did in my brother's case."

"What do you mean?"

"Well, I was a baby, but I heard that when my mom was working and we were sleeping, my brother was creeping…and that 'creeping' got him a baby or two. But nonetheless, in my eyes, it was still fun times growing up….until everyone started graduating from high school. Everyone was eager to move out and do their own thing. Of the eleven kids, six left right after graduation, doing everything from going to college, going to work, or starting their military careers, leaving the other five of us at home. Suddenly, the once crowded and boisterous, happy home environment was slowly becoming almost empty, almost silent… too quiet. It seemed like everyone was leaving, but we knew it was for the best. The fun part was visiting our siblings' new cribs. My oldest brother was the first to go. We were happy for him. He moved out and started his own family.

For us, his home was our little sanctuary, the best place to go while mom was working. And since I was the youngest at that time, his kids and I got along super fine because we were almost within the same age group. We would rotate between our other siblings every weekend until we were old enough to stay home by ourselves. And though we could stay home, we still took advantage of hanging with them, mainly my oldest brother. Spending the weekends with him and his family, there was never a dull moment. And as my brother's family expanded, I felt privileged to return the favor and help him out with his younger kids. So, as you can well imagine, my brother's house became the ideal hang out spot. This was a house full of teenagers and babies, a little 'man-joint', if you will, since it was mostly boys. I was just glad that I at least had someone close in age to hang with. My brother and sister-in-law Michelle had a few kids not long after I was born: the twins and my niece Tiana.

My niece and I were a few years apart but you would think we were sisters because of how close we were. We did everything together; man, we always had fun. Oh, how we loved hanging out with her dad (my brother) and his family. We always did things together. The neighborhood of Boyd Heights, where they lived, always came alive, especially on weekends. Party after party, back to back….all that went down in the neighborhood park. There was, however, one problem: my niece and I were too young to hang out or party, and we always had to beat those street lights before they came on, unless the older kids were hanging out and would watch us. Every weekend, we would ask to stay out a little later but the answer was always the same: 'Y'all know the routine; don't let the street lights catch ya!' Man, how we wished for a different answer just once. We always made it in on time though, lest we got a good old fashioned ass-whooping. We stayed out of trouble hoping that once, just once, my brother or Michelle would have a change of heart. Well, it happened. One weekend, with all the kids over my brother's house as usual, he decided he wanted to get his romance on and take Michelle out for the evening.

I felt uneasy about the arrangements at first. That meant no fun at the park tonight, we thought. But, as they got ready to walk out the door, Michelle called Tiana and me to the door but she looked directly at me and said "Girls, listen….We know you all like to stay out by the park with everybody and there's nothing to do in the house at this point, and since your brother and I are going out, we will allow you two to stay out just a little while longer, Oh, one thing though: just be home by ten, and, I mean ten; not ten 0' one… but ten!'

"Oh my gosh!" I blurted. She couldn't be serious; did I hear her correctly? Was I hearing voices? Michelle actually said we were allowed to stay out an extra two hours tonight! We thought we were in Heaven! To be given the privilege of staying out! Shit!, you couldn't tell us anything. We thought we were going to be the shit at

the park that night. All eyes were going to be on us. We couldn't wait..., hanging out with the crew, sitting in the bleachers, watching the guys play basketball, shoot dice, play dominos or spades, and listen to the big boys (dope boys) ride by or watch them park and profile in the parking lot with their fancy car tops rolled down and the trunk of their pricy cars flashed wide open, blasting loud pulsating music. We never needed a DJ, those guys were the DJ's. Then, there was Meka, the neighborhood boss chick who every young girl wanted to be like. You see, Meka was built like a stripper: Big tits, small waist and a big ass, not to mention her caramel complexion. Most women were paying for a body like Ms. Meka, but she was all-natural. It wasn't hard for her to make her presence known, and, of course, all the dope boys wanted her but knew they didn't have a chance because of Big Dred.

"Big Dred... who is Big Dred?" the doctor interrupted.

"I'll get to him in a minute; just be patient, Doc. Now... the best part of being able to hangout at the park

was the dance battles. They loved to see us coming; they all knew what was going to happen. Our standards were high, and we always met the crowd's expectations. My niece Tiana and I loved to dance. We would always draw a huge crowd. They would form a circle around us just to watch us dive at each other in some serious dance moves with other girls from the neighborhood. We were always so excited, not just to vaunt our latest body moves, but, finally, we would have our chance to mingle with the big dogs. We were in Utopia! But as we began walking closer to the park, we noticed the crowd growing bigger. Suddenly, a black, heavily tinted car screeched up beside us and stopped abruptly. The windows slowly rolled down and a husky voice chimed in,

"Damn Baby, what's up? What's ya name?"

Tiana and I eyed each other, not too sure how to respond, or, if we should.

Then another voice interrupted, laughing mockingly, "Big Dred, you better leave them little girls alone before they put yo ass under the jail!"

You see, Big Dred was an O.G. (original gangster) and Meka's boyfriend. He was the biggest dope boy in the neighborhood; everybody knew and 'respected' Meka and Big Dred. The only problem was that Big Dred spent more time in jail than on the streets…well, that's also another story.

So, as Big Dred ignored the laughter and yelling of his cohorts, he continued his conversation with us with a mischievous smirk on his face, 'Y'all need a ride? Y'all sliding to the park?' he asked inquisitively.

"Yeah, we are, but we have to walk," I responded.

"Oh, ok, see you later, Tiana!" Big Dred smiled and sped off. I asked her how he knew her name, but she ignored me and started hurrying away. I was very uneasy, but, I let it go…well, for a while. We finally made it to the park where everybody was watching the court. They were tuned into the b-ball game as usual until the music started. It was on and popping! Then, finally, it was time to get the party started; everyone stood and cheered in great anticipation of the popular showdown of talents. As the eager crowd grew, so did our egos. It was time to shut

the place down and showcase some turbulent dance moves.

My sister Tina, my brother Kenny and my nephew David didn't like it when we danced because they would always have to stop what they were doing and watch us. They said it was just too much of a distraction, especially the reaction of the older dudes who would stop what they were doing, jaws dropped, appearing to be in a trance. They couldn't concentrate on their basketball game anymore and everything came to a virtual standstill.

Kenny would come over yelling, 'What the hell, man… damn! Go home! We ain't got time to be out here babysittin' because y'all want to be grown. Take y'all fast asses home!'

We ignored them and kept on dancing, actually turning it up a notch. We kicked off our shoes and we kicked up a violent dancing storm like we were going to win a prize and a trophy at the end of the night. We danced so much that we lost track of time, but, we didn't care. And, by ignoring them, Kenny became mad, so, he said it again, only louder and more aggressively.

'It's nine-thirty; y'all, better take y'all asses home!'

We glanced at each other and realized that Kenny had just said nine-thirty, which meant we weren't going to make it home in time, but, we still had to try. At that moment, the party was over for us. We broke through the crowd and started our trek home. The journey seemed interminably long...taking forever, I guess because we were so upset; but, truth is, we didn't care because, again, we had left our footprints in the park. Our signature moves and dancing frenzy had become a part of the park's rich history; everyone looked forward to it, and we were not going to let anyone or anything take away from that. But, we weren't alone. Within seconds, the pipes echoed from the cherry red 1964 vintage drop-top convertible Chevy as it cruised and gradually came to a halt beside us.

The cool air and almost crisp Floridian breeze accommodated the pulsating music blasting deafeningly from the open trunk. 'Need a ride, Lil' Momma?' The last syllable had hardly left his mouth before Tiana

sprang into the front seat. Shocked, I wondered what to do. I was lost, and quite confused, because this dude had changed cars on us. I was standing there looking like boo-boo the fool cause I couldn't let her ride by herself, just standing in a trance thinking I'm damned if I do and damned if I don't. So, reluctantly, I hopped into the back seat, riding along with Meka's man, Big Dred. Man… was I scared. Tiana, on the other hand, was all too relaxed and comfortable, legs criss-crossed, a wild ear-to-ear grin and right arm hanging off the door, as if she owned his ride. She was owning that ride! There was no doubt that she had done this before."

"But, tell me, why do you feel like she was too comfortable, Jay?"

"Because she couldn't stop smiling and she seemed to know where everything was in his car. And, bear in mind, she already had a serious crush on this dude. Picture Big Dred…a tall, dark-skinned, handsome guy. He was a lady's man… unquestionably every woman's fantasy. Only problem: Big Dred was a 'womanizer'. Nothing is wrong with a man loving

women, or being pussy crazy, he just took it too far. He used the wrong 'head' to do everything. This dude had fifteen kids from eleven different women...and still counting, almost like a bag of skittles. He definitely had been tasting the rainbow because, the kids were all different races and varying heights. I couldn't understand what Tiana saw in him, but, whatever it was, she had difficulty resisting. I sat in that backseat mad as hell. I felt that this girl was going to get us beat to sleep when her mom or dad saw us getting out of this grown ass man's car, so I tried to play it off.

Tiana turned to the back seat and glanced at me and questioned, 'What's wrong, Auntie?'

The damn nerves she had.

"Nothing, Tiana." But, my facial expression told a whole different story. I couldn't say much anyway because all that heavy bass from all the different rap and hip-hop music was throbbing me in the back. He changed it though, and turned on some slow music as if he was trying to set the mood. I won't lie, this dude's car was a nice one, it really was but that didn't stop me from being mad at Tiana for being too comfortable with him.

The car came to a quick stop. "Why are we stopping?" I asked.

'This is our stop, Auntie. Now get out and give me a minute!'

"Get out? What you mean by get out? Heifer, what you mean? You better get your ass out and come on, man!"

'Just give me a minute, Auntie! Damn!'

"Well, I had no choice because he let me out of the car and I scrambled over to the sidewalk, shocked and confused. As I turned to wait for Tiana to alight from the car, I was in for a big surprise: I had become a spectator to the unthinkable playing out right in front of me! She was doing something I had yet to experience. This grown ass twenty-year old man was deep kissing my fifteen-year old niece…her lips, neck, ears….. I didn't know what to do; I was in total shock. I couldn't even take my eyes off them, not because I wanted some, but because I was scared about what would probably happen next. I was really surprised that she would attempt this right before my eyes! As he stuck his tongue into her mouth and grabbed the back of her head pulling her closer, kissing her last breath, I couldn't react. I thought it was a real hot love scene from a movie. Catching her breath, Tiana reluctantly shuffled her way out of the car. He then handed her a stack of money and told her he'd call her later. Smiling from ear to ear, she dragged herself towards me, in a daze, and asked me one of the dumbest questions in the world."

'What? What Auntie?'

"What you mean, what? First of all, heifer, you cussed at me, secondly, we are not home yet, and thirdly, is there something you want to tell me? What the hell is really going on? How did that happen?"

"Chile, that's just my friend, he knows I like him but he said I'm just too young."

"Well, I couldn't tell, the way you two were sucking on each other. Too young my ass."

"I told him to give me a few more years and I'm coming for him. He's really just looking out for me. That's all."

"That's all, oh, really? Ok, Tiana, you better know what you're doing. I'm not taking any ass whoopin' because I knew about you and this dude. By the way, how much money did he give you? Where's my cut or I'm telling, and you better be careful. So, we had to hurry up and run since his punk ass dropped us off round the corner. Let's go!"

We dashed around the corner so fast that we were out of breath by the time we reached home. Sweaty, heart palpitating, we caught our breaths and whispered in hushed tones. "Woo, we made it. With a minute left to spare." I chimed in mockingly.

"Dang track star, you out of shape. Can't even catch your breath, oh, my bad… you just getting old. Hurry up and open the door, he supposed to be calling me tonight. So I need to get in, eat, and take my shower before he calls." She boasted.

I couldn't believe my ears. My niece was falling for this man, who, in my opinion, was only out for one thing. Damn she was desperate! But I prayed that she would find that out in due time.

'Mmm….Mmm….was my nose deceiving me? Man something smelled good coming from the kitchen,' I opened the front door and the aroma smacked me. I wondered what it could be. My cousin Sonia was up in that kitchen feeding the other kids and I couldn't wait to get a plate.

"Sonia, what's that you cooked? Can we eat?"

"In a minute,' she assured, just waiting on the bread to finish. You all go wash your hands."

"I don't need any bread, fix my plate, please."

Sonia wasn't having it, she stopped in mid scoop, turned and yelled, "I said go wash ya damn hands."

I immediately ran to the bathroom to attempt to do just that, however it was impossible. Tiana was already in there with the door locked, shower running and the music blasting. This girl was really trying to get herself together before that dude was supposed to call. This seemed to be a normal routine for Tiana, but I didn't care. I was hungry and I was not going to get yelled at again, so I began bamming on the door for Tiana to unlock it so I could get in. Man it was almost eleven 0' clock and I was starving. Finally when Tiana opened the door, I didn't even have time to argue at this point I just wanted to wash up and go eat so I pushed her aside and did just that. I then made my way back up the hallway headed to the kitchen when a loud boom stopped me dead in my tracks. Sonia and I were both just standing there trying to figure out where the noise was coming from. Brushing it off we both headed back to the kitchen to grab our plate and head to the couch. Well, as Sonia got ready to hand me my plate, the doorbell rang, then the phone started ringing too.

"Come in, I mean who is it?" I said.

"Hello! What! Girl, when?' Sonia asked the caller on the line.

Just then the door flew open and all we heard was, 'Sonia, girl, turn on the news!

Terry, the neighborhood 'go-to' girl for all the juicy gossip, lies, stories and neighborhood drama was coming in with her usual story to tell, but this time though, it was different, she had proof. The words 'BREAKING NEWS' flashed across the TV screen corroborated her story.

Standing in front of the TV I flopped down on the couch from the news with my plate in hand. The news was reporting that a local drug bust had gone bad, leaving two dead and one injured. We all sat there, solemnly watching the TV, while the sirens continued their relentless wailing, ambulances and Fire Rescue were creating a cacophony of musical confusion outside. Tiana was standing in the hallway with this look of fear on her face; she was praying she wouldn't hear those dreadful words from the newscast. And, to think that Big Dred had just dropped us off less than an hour ago, so we had all reasons to be concerned, Tiana especially. So as we sat there in disbelief, trying to ascertain the names of the victims. We couldn't believe this was happening and kept belaboring the point that we had just seen them at the block party.

As the news anchor began calling the names of the deceased, we froze. I turned and looked at Tiana's face to see her reaction, but I ended up doing a double take because the third name that was called was too familiar, he was injured, this injured person was…Derric Patson a.k.a. Big Dred. Tiana's sigh of relief changed instantly to worry and panic. The only problem was, she couldn't tell anyone.

"Thank God!" I mumbled, then immediately got up and began walking towards my niece.

"Ah, Tiana, Thank God, he's alive!"

Although it was good news, in a sense, everyone else was talking about how he was fucked up. I couldn't believe what I was hearing because he had Tiana and me in the car, riding around, and, from what we were hearing, Big Dred was carrying so much weed and drugs, in addition to six pistols and countless ammunition. Just thinking, how the hell would we have been able to explain that one to my brother and Tiana's mom. Then I truly understood why everyone was saying he was fucked up. Rumor was rife that it was his third strike and he was already on probation, and, to add trafficking with intent to sell on his record, man, this dude was done! He certainly could not use his 'get out of jail' card on this one, because he was on Federal Probation. So, you know what that meant, Big Dred was headed back up the road....straight to prison.

Tiana and I stood in the hallway trying not to make sense of the obvious, she couldn't believe it. Just like that and it was over, her dear friend had been taken into custody. She couldn't take it anymore, and as I watched my niece race back into her room with tear-filled eyes, I quickly followed. I knocked frantically on the door,

"Tiana, Tiana...are you o.k.?" I whispered as I entered.

"What's up, auntie?

Why are you crying, you want to talk about it?" I pleaded.

"No, I'm ok. I'll just lay here and wait for his call,' she assured.

Now Doc, I don't pretend to be the smartest person in the world, but if facial expressions were really worth a thousand words, or, if you could have read my mind, you would have been just as lost, confused and clueless as I was. I really wanted to punch my niece in the back of the head in that same exact spot he grabbed her when he kissed her earlier, and yell,

Hey, dumb ass! That dude ain't thinking about you. Wake up! Dummy, that could have been us in the car with him! I thought to myself. And, truth is, that's what I really wanted to say, instead, I kept my comments to myself. I couldn't help but wonder what it was about that man that fascinated her and had her 'in her feelings' this way. Man, I didn't understand, here was this naïve fifteen year old girl who didn't have a clue of what was going on, and madly in love with someone she could never have. She wasn't even sure she would ever see this man again. Damn…poor Tiana.

Chapter 2

The ride on the prison bus seemed like eternity. All Big Dred had in his thoughts was being fucked up again. Due to his probation violation, the judge revoked his bond and gave him thirty-six months (3 years) for the new charges. Big Dred was feeling betrayed, upset and alone because of the things that had happened and the people with whom he had associated himself. His life had changed in an instant. Of course, his main chick, Ms. Meka was long gone with his money. Also, every nigga known to man that had his phone number that he was running around with had changed their numbers or had put a block on the line. And don't even mention visitation…that was out of the question! His mind was just running wild.

As the bus rolled onto the compound, the huge, iron gates slowly pried open and the machine moved in menacingly and then came to an abrupt stop. Big Dred took a long look out the window, wishing he could have taken back those last few moments, moments that would ultimately cost him his freedom for the next thirty-six months.

"Count time! Remain in your seats, I repeat, remain in your seats!" The correctional officer ordered.

After giving this long speech and directions on how this transport was about to take place, Big Dred became weak and very ill. Finally able to get off the bus, the inmates who were shackled with Big Dred became his guide. Then the correctional officer yelled,

"Stay in line and head towards the area that is marked Receiving/Discharge!"

Big Dred was not happy about that at all, he was even more pissed off that he got no sympathy for being ill, and on top of that, having to go through this ordeal once again. As the gang of inmates made their way up the sidewalk, they were greeted in front of the Receive/Discharge entrance by the institution's warden, the doctor and a nurse.

The warden gave a brief speech to the new inmates, "These were the people in charge of giving you your physical exams, as well as getting you processed for access to the compound and to receive your permanent housing assignment." The warden said as he pointed at the two.

"Hello, gentlemen, I am Dr. White and this is nurse Melon. We will be taking it from here. Open R/D #1! Single file up against the wall." Dr. White ordered.

As the inmates made their way inside the R/D office, the space got smaller and smaller.

"Close R/D #1!" The nurse instructed.

"Now, is everybody in? Ok, listen closely as I will only give these instructions once."

The process had begun. Big Dred's mind began to wander again as he fell into a daze, he felt worse. At that moment, reality was setting in. The doctor and the nurse were trying to give instructions when Big Dred started yelling.

"Nurse!' He shouted. "I need to lie down!"
"Excuse me,' she said. "Lie down, what's wrong with you?"

"I'm not feeling well. Please, I need to lie down."

As the nurse approached him, she read his name tag, 'Patson....Patson, where's Patson's paperwork? Sit in this chair for now until I get you checked in. Better yet, I'll have you lay in this holding cell until it's your turn to be examined by Dr. White. C.O. (Correctional Officer) uncuff him please, and put him in cell two bunk one for now."

Hours had passed as each inmate went through the proper procedures and exam as they were now official property of the F.B.P. Big Dred was lying down restlessly on his bunk when he heard, "Patson #55569-123!"

"Yeah!" he bellowed reluctantly.

"Let's go! You're next, time for your exam and to see where we will be placing you."

"What you mean? Shit, general population."

"Yeah, but not here, slick, since you know everything your ass should have known that this place is temporary. It just determines where your permanent stay will be," she reminded sarcastically.

"Well, how am I supposed to know that nurse?"

"Really? Are you serious? Now you know, mister, this is not new to you. Your paperwork shows that, well….it's not your first time, or, as you young people call it, your first rodeo," she said mockingly.

"So, what now, what's next?"

"You know the routine. First things first, let me get a urine sample, blood work, and then a full physical will be done. And when the doctor finishes the exam, it will be processed, sent out and you'll go back to your cell.

When the labs come back, you will probably still be in orientation but you will be contacted and placed from there. So, let's get started.

After the physical was complete, Big Dred began to head back to the holding cell when Nurse Melon realized that he wasn't joking.

"From the look of things, this man wasn't faking, he was really sick. He was running a temperature, accompanied by pockets of sweat all over his forehead and other parts of his body, his pressure was up and he was complaining of a headache."

Nurse Melon gave him a cool, soaked washcloth to put on his forehead, an aspirin and a glass of water.

"I can't give you too much until I know all your allergies and we go over your previous medical chart again," she advised. "For now, just go back to your bunk and rest."

"Thank you, Nurse Melon," Dred said gratefully, "You're welcome," she replied.

A couple of days went by and Big Dred began to feel better, not only was he finally feeling better but he was now on the compound in general population with the other 1996 inmates. Trying to re-adapt to the life he thought he'd left behind, he tried to find something to do. He decided he'd walk around the compound to see if anything had changed since his last incarceration five years ago. To his surprise, it seemed that not much had really changed at all, inmates were still playing cards, gambling, shootin' dice, lifting weights, playing basketball with a vicious competition as if they were in the NBA, and telling a whole lot of yearbook tales, (bullshit ass back in the day war and women stories; the 'what I had back in 1999' kinda bull), well, you get the picture.

Continuing to stroll the compound Big Dred decided to head out to the Recreation aka Rec Yard to walk the track. He still had a lot on his mind now that he was alone; and, now that the smoke had cleared he had no one in his corner....no one. As Big Dred walked the track he began daydreaming, all he had on his mind was that young pretty Lil' thick chocolate chick that he called Lil' Mama. The one that was crazy about him even though he really couldn't or wouldn't give her the time of day because she was too young in the first place.

Tiana, Tiana was on his mind heavily. All he was thinking about is how he could get in touch with her without anyone suspecting anything. He also wondered if he was even still thought of since it had been several months since he did his disappearing act, vanishing without a trace.

Big Dred wanted to call someone to help him get in touch with Tiana, but, who? Who could he get to accept his call since the whole world had turned its back on him completely? There was only one number that he knew that would definitely pick up and accept the charges. Guess...his momma! His momma was the only person that no matter how bad things had gotten; she was always in his corner. Well, I guess that's what mommas are supposed to do. So, Big Dred mustered the courage and decided to give it a shot. He headed back to the unit and hurried to the pay phone. As he was about to make the call, he realized that he only had a few minutes before chow, so he had to make it quick.

After about three seconds of ringing,

"Hello!"

"You have a collect call from Derric Patson. Hang up now or press seven to decline the call. If you would like to accept the call, press five now or say yes after the tone."

"Yes! Hello, Derric!"

"Momma, hey ma!" he screamed excitedly.

"Wow, you finally decided to call and it's only been four months."

"I know momma, I just been going through it."

"I know son, I know, but you could have called me just to let me know you were ok. I was so worried, but thank you Jesus you alright. So, how you been?"

Big Dred didn't realize how much he missed hearing his momma's voice that he totally forget what he was calling her for. He was just listening with a smile on his face. They talked the entire fifteen minutes and he promised to call home more often before the call was disconnected. He hadn't smiled like that in months, finally he had someone who would reassure him that he wasn't forgotten, that he still existed and was loved dearly. The call ended and he hung the phone up and headed to chow. After chow was complete, Big Dred noticed that he was starting to feel sick again. He became very tired; he felt weak and exhausted. He was so exhausted that he skipped calling his mom back and went straight to his bunk, lay down and went to sleep.

For the next few weeks, Big Dred's health fluctuated, he became curious and really wanted to know why he kept feeling ill. He knew he was good because he never heard back from Dr. White or Nurse Melon for that matter. But he was concerned because now, along with fatigue, exhaustion, the cold and constant coughing, he kept throwing up and suffered severe loss of appetite, he was also having headaches on a regular basis.

"Sounds a bit familiar to me," interrupted doc.

Big Dred would find himself in and out of bed all day, some days he wouldn't get out of bed at all. He felt bad, those headaches just wouldn't quit. He kept trying to figure out what was wrong and thought to himself,

Damn man, what the hell is going on? I know damn well none of those slick hoes not pregnant. Today makes five months since I've been gone, so, I know no hoe can trick me. Man, I need to go to medical in the morning.

He sat in silence; thinking, wondering, sighing…then he arose and decided to call it a night. He went back to sleep.

'Morning count time, count time!' Big Dred heard the guard shout as usual. But he was feeling so bad that he couldn't even get out of bed. He knew this feeling wasn't normal so, as soon as count was complete and cleared, he headed to Medical to see Dr. White. He entered the medical office just in time as Nurse Melon was finishing up with an inmate.

"Sign in and have a seat, I'll be with you shortly."

As Big Dred attempted to sign in, he began to feel nauseous. Trying to make it to the chair, he started throwing up again, then collapsed and hit the floor with a thud.

"Nuuuuurse, Nurse Melon!" an inmate shouted.

At that moment Big Dred's life flashed before his very eyes.

"Code blue….code blue! I need an E.T.A. (estimated time arrival) on the Paramedics." Nurse Melon yelled over the handheld radio.

A response was received almost immediately.

"Paramedics are on the compound, five minutes away."

"Don't touch him, nobody touch him." Another voice yelled.

And as Nurse Melon ran to his aid, she realized Big Dred was unresponsive and was face down in his vomit. She tried to turn him over, but, just as she placed her hand on his shoulder, Dr. White advised her to step back as the paramedics were entering the building. The stretcher was carefully laid out and they proceeded to position Big Dred. Then Nurse Melon tried to bring the EMT in charge up to speed with all information pertaining to Dred.

Big Dred's lab work and test results hadn't returned as yet, this was a red flag, they knew something wasn't right.

Securing him on the stretcher and gathering his medical release form, the paramedics were now on their way to the nearby hospital with Big Dred fighting for his life. They made several attempts to revive him but he remained unconscious and unresponsive. They tried everything to stabilize Big Dred, one paramedic placed an oxygen mask on his face and began to pump oxygen into his body, while another one of the paramedics took his vitals and got his I.V. started so that he would be thoroughly prepped upon their arrival at the hospital.

And, just as the paramedics pulled into the emergency entrance, they noticed the trauma unit team was waiting. The doors of the ambulance swung open and the trauma team sprang into action.

The charge nurse began with the usual questions, "What's the problem? Bring us up to speed, Name: Derric Patson, paperwork, is this the inmate?" She asked,

"Yes it is," the EMT replied.

"I'll take it from here."

The charge nurse and her staff continued administering CPR when they realized he was still handcuffed to the stretcher, so, they had security carefully remove the cuffs so that they could maneuver with no encumbrances. One, two, three, four, five," the nurse counted as she pumped his chest. More pressure…still, nothing.

"Is the defibrillator ready? Hand me the paddles, ready….clear!" His body jumped from the shock, but still nothing significant.

"Hit it again, ready…Clear!"

Suddenly, life re-entered his body and Big Dred took a quick breath, then another, followed by other short, small breaths. Finally, he was breathing, albeit with the help of the oxygen tubes, and, he was trying to speak. In a daze, he squinted his eyes and peeped around, trying to make sense of this unusual place. He continued taking these short, shallow breaths, then he asked, "Where am I?"

"Derric, can you hear me?' The nurse whispered.

'Do you know where you are?" He nodded from side to side.

"No?'

'Is that a no?' she verified his nodding.

"Well, you are in the hospital. Westsung Memorial Hospital."

Still confused, Big Dred just lay there staring blankly at the ceiling. He was still trying to figure out what had happened and why he was there, he remained in a state of confusion, glancing around at intervals and occasionally shaking his head. The nurses tried to keep him calm and relaxed and explained to him that he had passed out at the institution, and that he was subsequently brought there for treatment.

'Just relax and rest, we're going to continue to get you prepped to begin a battery of tests and get these fluids in your body because you are dehydrated. We'll talk a little later and answer any questions you may have, but, for now, just rest.'

Big Dred didn't respond, perhaps he wasn't understanding very well, but he just nodded his head affirmatively, closed his eyes and fell into deep slumber. As the early morning sun began to crack through the tiny window blinds, there was a knock at the door.

"Mr. Patson, Good Morning! I'm Dr. Vargas and I'll be overseeing you and your treatment while you are with us. Can you tell me what happened?"

By this time, Big Dred was able to open his eyes, breathe a little better and answer a few basic questions.

"Sir, I really don't remember anything. I just remember trying to sign in at the infirmary for treatment. Next thing I know I woke up here, handcuffed to this stretcher, with a bunch of strange faces staring at me."

"Well, tell me how you feel?"

"I'm weak, but I'm ok, I guess. Do you know what's wrong with me, Doc?"

"Not sure yet, Mr. Patson, but looking at your chart and your history, I have to ask you this, did you know you were diabetic?"

"No!"

"Well, we're running a few tests, as well as attempting to revive your strength and return your pressure to normal, then you will be released into the care of the institution."

Big Dred was in shock, he didn't know what was going on, and this couldn't be good.

'Diabetes? He thought….what the hell? wonder if momma knew this BS and didn't tell me.'

He wanted to call her to find out but that wasn't happening because as he began to call for assistance, the door swung open and a guard stomped in.

"Hello Patson…I'm Officer Sims and I'll be here with you until you are released. Your mother has been notified and she hopes you're ok."

He inquired curiously, "When will she be allowed to come to see me?" Big Dred asked.

"Come see you, hmm… see you where? Here, oh, not here. That will never happen. But she will be given updates and once you return to the institution then you can make contact. So, for now, all you can do is eat, take your meds, meditate, rest and wait."

Big Dred realized that this guard wasn't playing so he had no choice but to listen and cooperate. For the next few days it was the same thing, he ate, took his meds, watched TV, allowed his mind to wander… and slept. And, as the hours began to roll by on the sixth day, Big Dred was becoming frustrated. It had been six days of boredom. Six frustrating days, he didn't have any idea of what was going on with the outside world. He wanted to get up and move around, but, before he knew it, the five o' clock major news was on the screen.

"Knock knock…Mr. Patson, it's me, I'm coming in!" Dr. Vargas announced as he entered the room.

"How are you feeling? Ready to go? All your tests came back fine. Cat scan, X-rays and the MRI are showing no signs of trauma. So, I'm discharging you. You're being discharged, son. Your pressure is down and back to normal. Your vitals are good. You just need to change your diet and educate yourself on diabetes.

Diabetes is a disease that will not kill you like that, but at the same time, it should not be taken lightly."

"Wait, that's all? Big Dred interrupted, his eyes beaming, 'that's all you have to say to me?"

"What were you expecting?"

"Well, with all the tests you all ran you would think it was more than that. I thought I was dying!'

"Well, sir, to be perfectly honest, you were in shock when you came in, my staff revived you, you were treated for a concussion and your pressure was off the charts, but we did what had to be done to get things back to normalcy for you.

The institution will continue to monitor you and do a follow up as necessary since you belong to them. Also, Dr. White at the institution will be the one administer anymore tests or labs if necessary. Just be grateful it wasn't worse. And take care of yourself."

Meanwhile, back at the Institution….Dr. White and Nurse Melon were in the office conducting physicals and distributing meds when the phone rang.

"Hello, Medical Intake Nurse Melon, how may I assist you?"

"Hello, Nurse Melon, this is Nurse Gloria Spring from Westsung Memorial Hospital and I'm calling about a discharge. Inmate Derric Patson #55569-123 is in the process of being discharged, you may send transportation now."

"Ok, Nurse Spring, will do, I will set that up now."

"Can you give me an E.T.A. Nurse Spring asked?

"Sure, give me a minute, standby please."

"Ok, thank you." As Nurse Melon entered Big Dred's information into the system, a message alert popped up, *SPECIAL HOUSING, SPECIAL HOUSING (Medical Unit)* Nurse Melon immediately called the Special Housing/Medical Unit quad to see if a bunk would be available for the arrival of Inmate Patson, unfortunately there was none. Nurse Melon was given assurance that everything would be handled and ready within a few more days, he would be fine in the holding cell until the bunk was up to standard for him to move in.

"Ok, I'll send his belongings including his chart over now. Everything is sealed and on its way."

"We'll be on the look out for it." So the Special Housing (Medical Unit) prepared for Inmate Patson's arrival and the guards at the hospital continued to guard the room.

Suddenly a nurse from the nurse's station requested that one of the guards come see her immediately.

"Here, officer you have a phone call."

"Thank you, Officer Christian speaking."

"This is the reception desk downstairs, your transportation has arrived."

"Ok, thanks, appreciate it." And just like that, Big Dred was packed up, placed in shackles, placed in a wheelchair and escorted down the service elevator for departure.

As they began the ride back to the institution, Big Dred remained quiet just staring out the window, daydreaming. Still not feeling one hundred percent, he couldn't help but become a little agitated and impatient because he couldn't wait to get to a phone to call his mother. You see, Big Dred was finally ready to reach out to Tiana and knew his mother would be willing to do anything to help her son make that happen. But as the van pulled into the institution, he further noticed that they were headed in a different direction.

"Excuse me Officer, what's up? Where are we headed?" Big Dred questioned

"Just sit back and ride, you've been reassigned."
"Reassigned? Oh ok. Will this be my permanent housing?"

"Not sure, I don't know. We're just doing our job. You'll get a chance to talk to your counselor when you get inside."

As the van stopped in front of the new building and Big Dred noticed two people waiting at the gate to greet them. He also wondered where he was and why he was being brought way out in the middle of nowhere, far away from civilization, far from the original institution.

The doors to the van were unlocked and he glanced outside and immediately noticed that the two individuals who were waiting to welcome him was an officer and a nurse, but, not the ones with whom he has familiar. This was a different nurse than the one before, this was not Nurse Melon, he thought.

"Inmate Patson!" the nurse shouted.

"Yeah! I mean Yes!" he replied.

"I am Nurse Savoy and I will be completing the process for you to enter this compound and close out your hospital release. Understand?"

"Ma'am, please, quick question…what happened to Nurse Melon?"

"Please exit the vehicle and state your full name and inmate number."

"Derric Patson #55569-123!"

"Ok, sir, follow me." Nurse Savoy instructed. As they began walking up the sidewalk, Big Dred tried asking questions about his new residence and the former nurse, but was quickly cut off by Nurse Savoy.

"No talking, Thank you! Open R/D one!"

And the doors slid open for them to enter the intake room. Nurse Savoy gave instructions and moved fast. Finally the shackles and handcuffs were removed and Big Dred was ushered into a tiny cell.

"Patson, please don't get too comfortable,' the nurse rudely advised, 'you'll be moving to a dorm with your bunk assignment shortly."

"Ok, thank you, but I have a question. When will I be able to use the phone?"

"Tomorrow. Just wait until tomorrow. For now, just get some rest and you'll have access to the phones tomorrow. Have a good night, Mr. Patson."
The next morning the compound wake up alarm sounded, Big Dred just lay there. He had no idea what to do, he had nowhere to go, so he just stayed in bed. All of a sudden his name was blasting over the intercom, 'Patson, Derric Patson please report to the desk.' Surprised he jumped up, put his slides on and headed into the hall. While passing, an Officer approached him and asked, "Hey, are you Patson?" "Yes, I am. What's up?" Big

Dred replied. "Did you not hear your name being called?" "I heard it, yes sir.

That's where I'm heading to right now but I didn't know what desk I am supposed to report to."

The officer just stared at him and commanded, 'follow me.'

"Ok, but where am I going?"

"Just follow me and all your questions will be answered sooner than you imagine."

As they continued down this long hallway, Big Dred noticed a lot of offices. Soon they approached this one particular door and Big Dred noticed the sign read, 'Mrs. C. Cameron, Counselor,' on it.

"Counselor!" Big Dread yelled. Why am I here?" He demanded.

"I don't know, Patson, I was just asked to escort you here." The officer replied while knocking on the door.

"Knock knock"

"Come in!"

"Mrs. Cameron, this is Inmate Patson. Inmate Patson this is Counselor, Mrs. Cameron."

"Do, come in, have a seat."

"Thank you, Officer."

"Mr. Patson, don't you want to sit down?"

"No thank you, what's going on?' He was getting very agitated. 'Why am I here?"

"We're waiting on Nurse Savoy so we can begin."

"Nurse Savoy! Man, what's up? Tell me now!" Big Dred shouted.

"Is it my momma, one of my kids, what? Tell me what's going on." He was getting quite furious and it was obvious in his voice.

"Excuse me, Mr. Patson, there's no need to shout. Nurse Savoy and I will explain just as soon as she gets here."

They were interrupted by a loud knocking on the door.

"Mrs. Cameron."

"Come on in, Nurse Savoy!"

As Nurse Savoy entered the room, Big Dred became more antsy and irritated.

"Ok, here we are now, so, tell me what the hell is going on?' Big Dred continued to demand a response.

"Hey, hey….calm down, Mr. Patson." This is proper protocol and correct procedure. Now, have a seat."

"Nah, I'm good,' he assured, 'just talk to me."

"Ok, Mr. Patson, the reason for this meeting is to inform you of the reason you are being placed at this location. Please adhere to the guidelines, rules and regulations of this compound and institution."

"In the counselor's office!" he interjected.

"Yes, sir, in the counselor's office,' he repeated.

"No disrespect ma'am, but I've been to prison before, and not once have I ever gone through orientation like this."

"Well, sir, that's not anything to be proud of or brag about, but just to let you know this time is different. Now, if I may continue…Mr. Derric Patson #55569-123 is this correct?"

"Yes!"

"This is the Federal Bureau of Prison's Medical Facility and you have been transferred to this compound from regular population due to your medical needs. Inmates are housed here to be monitored and maintain a healthy lifestyle. This will be your permanent residence for the duration of your incarceration." Nurse Savoy went on and on about the guidelines, rules and regulations so much that Big Dred tuned her out.

This was no college course and he was not preparing for an exam so he didn't see the need to be tortured by her unnecessary harangue. Then, the most important part missed him.

"Patson!" she shouted. He jumped.

"Did you hear me?"

"Hear what?"

"Did you hear what I just said to you?" "Yeah, yeah, I heard you,' he lied.

"What did I say then?"

With a blank look on Big Dred's face he couldn't find the words to say. When asked to repeat what was said he became defensive.

"You said, ah man, you said…damn, man, just give me a break, I heard you!"

"Mr. Patson, now is not the time to be defensive or use inappropriate language, watch your mouth. We're here to help you through this."

"Help me through what?"

"I thought you said you heard me."

"Listen, Mr. Patson, I've had just about enough of the B.S. from you this morning. Now, I'll say this one more time, so, I'd advise you to listen so you will know what's wrong, how your treatments will go and how the pill line works for you.

"Treatment, pills…man they already told me I'm diabetic when I was in the hospital. So, just tell me what's next. I didn't realize diabetes was this bad."

"Mr. Patson, I will say it again, please pay attention and listen to me. Yes, it is true that you are a diabetic and you were notified by the hospital. But what you didn't know is that your lab test results came back as well while you were out. You missed the other part of orientation when we spoke to everyone so that's why you are here today. Now, I'll say it again, and just as Nurse Savoy started talking again, Big Dred tuned her out still standing there with a blank look on his face.

"Mr. Patson, Mr. Patson. Nurse Savoy said. 'Are you ok?" "Yeah, yeah, I'm ok."

"Did you hear me, you know what? I'm done. You're not even paying attention to anything I just said to you again.

I tell you what...when you're ready to give me your undivided attention, you come find me. Mrs. Cameron, good day."

Nurse Savoy grabs her things and hastily exits the office as Big Dred tried to stop her, but that was all in vain.

"I'm listening! I'm listening now! I'm sorry, I got a lot on my mind.''

'Oh, well, me too, but that's not stopping me from doing my job. And, at this point, I have other inmates to check on and distribute meds to. So, as I said before, when you're ready to give me your full attention you come see me. I don't have time for games, sir."

"Mr. Patson, please, please have a seat.' Miss Cameron firmly instructed. 'I need to give you the rest of the paperwork so you can fill it out and make sure you understand since you missed the orientation when you were in the hospital. After I'm done, then you can try and catch up with Nurse Savoy."

"But what was she saying, what's the big deal?"

"Your health and your well being are important. You should have paid attention. I'm so disappointed in your actions Mr. Patson, you need help. Stop being bitter and cut out the nonchalant behavior. That's no way for a grown man to behave.

You need to care more about yourself, love yourself and protect yourself if you really need others to help you. You have two and a half more years here, make it work for you. We are not the enemy. You did this to yourself.'

"Sorry, ma'am, I just got a lot on my mind."

"Well, at this point, that's not my concern. But you need to get it together, sir."

"Damn, y'all acting like diabetes will kill me."

"Really Mr. Patson?!"

"Ok, now I'm angry. Let me hurry up with this paperwork so you can get out of my office!' She began fumbling through the paperwork while shaking her head in disgust. Mrs. Cameron's speech went on for another frustrating forty-five minutes about the institution as a whole. And after all was said and done, she hurried up and released him.

"Mr. Patson, I do hope that you're headed up to Medical. You really need to go see Nurse Savoy."

'Ok, I will,' he agreed as he left her office. So, he moved toward the Medical building, and, perhaps not surprisingly, there he saw many of his home boys emerging from the dorms and heading out to the Rec. yard.

'Big Dred!' Someone shouted.

'What's up, man? You finally out on the compound?"

"Yeah, what's good, homie?"

"Out here to whip these dudes in dominos. Where you going?"

"Medical, trying to track down Nurse Savoy."

With a disconcerting look on his face, "Nurse Savoy, what you looking for her for?" he asked puzzled.

"She tried giving me my lab results but we kind of had it out in the other counselor Mrs. Cameron's office."

'Man, you know who Nurse Savoy she is?' shaking his head.

"No," Big Dred said.

His homeboy just kept looking away trying not to get in Big Dred's business.

"Never mind.' He replied.

Anyways, medical is closed until after lunch."

"Man, for real, damn!"

"Oh, well, you might as well come out to rec."

"'Y'all playing for money?" "You know it." "Shit cool, let's do it."

So, they headed it out and for the next few hours that was their hang-out spot. So, since Big Dred mentioned to his homie that he was on his way to Nurse Savoy, it put a red flag in the back of his mind. Knowing Big Dred didn't have a clue of who Nurse Savoy was, and he did, you know the first thing that everybody was thinking, well, you couldn't blame them, could you? But it wasn't any of his business, so he avoided the subject and instead, tried making small conversation while playing dominos. They stayed out on the rec yard so long that they missed lunch. Then one of the officers hit the intercom with the warning that it was almost count time, so they knew it was time to go. While walking back to the unit, the conversations kept them occupied and so Big Dred's mind was kept thinking about positive things. His homeboy couldn't wait to get to the phone to call his girl to see what the word on the street was about Big Dred, if anybody was talking. Because if they weren't they would be when he finished telling the news he had just found out. Now as they stepped into the unit heading their separate ways, Big Dred realized that he forgot to go to Nurse Savoy.

"Damn! I forgot. Oh well, I'll go in the morning. Guess I'll get my stuff together to take my shower."

He gathered his thoughts and his things to take a shower, then he began hearing some sounds, very weird noises like fire crackers coming from the ceiling. It sounded as if the ceiling was cracking and about to collapse. Still, Big Dred thought nothing of it. But, just as the count was cleared, he grabbed his toiletries and dashed to the shower.

Halfway down the hall in the unit he heard a loud explosion, something had collapsed. The sirens blasted relentlessly and the evacuation message was blaring through the loud speaker, "EVACUATE! EVACUATE! EVACUATE!"

What do I do?, Big Dred pondered to himself. As the halls starting accumulating dust and debris, there was nowhere to turn. All of a sudden Big Dred felt something, he couldn't move. He was trapped, something was pinning him down and thwarting his mobility and affecting his breathing. He couldn't figure out what huge, heavy object had him nailed to the ground.

"Help! help! help! I can't breathe!" He wailed.

But no one could hear him. He was almost sure that he was going to die right there and no one would find him. He screamed until he blacked out, clinging to life, hoping someone would come to his rescue. As the dust and debris got worse, his breathing became weaker and weaker, he began gasping for air until he became disoriented and eventually lost consciousness.

Was this the end of Big Dred? With all that he was dealing with, would this be the way God intended for him to leave this earth?

Chapter 3

It was Tiana's sixteenth birthday and she was ready to turn up for the weekend.

"Morning Daddy!"

"Morning Princess. Are you ready for a day full of surprises?"

"Yes, Daddy, yes; I can't wait for the party! Where's Momma?"

"Downstairs waiting on you so the pampering can begin."

"Pampering?"

"Yes, baby, your hair, nails and makeup, you're my princess, right?"

"Yes, Daddy, of course."

"Well, get on down those stairs before your mom starts screaming. I want this day to be so special for you; I want you to enjoy all that it has to offer. The biggest surprise I have will be given to you later on tonight."

"A big surprise, tonight? What is it, Daddy?"

"Now, if I tell you, it wouldn't be a surprise, right?"

"Just enjoy it all, it's your day, Princess. I love you."

"I Love you too, Daddy."

"Morning Momma!"

"Morning Birthday Girl. How'd you sleep?"

"Ok, I guess. I was too excited to sleep. I've been up trying to figure out how the party is going to be."

"Well, no need to worry. You know and I know that it will be a success, so stop stressing. Your daddy and I went all out, we over and beyond for this event and we spared no expense for you. Hey, you only turn sixteen once, so just enjoy it to the fullest. Now, come on, let's get started; you have a full day ahead of you."

"What time is my Auntie Jay coming?"

"Jay's on her way now. Well, I think she's on her way."

"Well how is everything else coming along…the venue and decorations?"

"Man, Tiana baby…everything is gorgeous, and the cake. Oh my, it was nice, beautiful, simply beautiful."

"Really, Momma?"

"Yes, Baby."

"Oh, my gosh, I'm so ready!"

"Well, don't rush it, just take it all in. These will be your memories for a lifetime, Baby. All I want is this: for you to be happy and enjoy. But honestly, I think we're all a lil' more excited than you are about this party."

'Knock, knock, coming in, Auntie Jay in the house and I'm ready to turn up! Where's the birthday girl?'

"I'm right here, Auntie Jay, in the kitchen with my momma."

'Well, I guess I better join ya'll then, huh? Where's the crew? Are they on their way?'

"Yes ma'am, they are supposed to be on they're way."

"Well at this point, right now I don't really care, the focus is on you. Gotta make sure that your outfit is on point and is making a statement. You and your girls need to set it off, get crunk and turn up tonight! Everything is in place for you to enjoy your Sweet 16 Baby Girl.'

"I just hope she has a good time."

'She will.' "I know I will. I'm just super excited because Daddy said he has a big surprise for me."

'A surprise?'

"Yes, Auntie Jay. Momma, do you know what it is?" Tiana inquired inquisitively.

'Now, why would I spoil the surprise?' she mused.

'Yes, I know. But I tell you what….you better come on and let's get started; before the rest of the girls get here.'

(A knock on the door) Knock, knock! "Knock, knock, coming in. Tiana, where you at?"

'We in the kitchen.'

"Heeey! Party time! What's up Birthday Girl? That hair and those nails are starting to look good. But it's about time to start getting dressed."

"Not quite, I still gotta get my make-up done. Just chill."

'But I'm ready to get dressed.'

"Me too, but we all gotta get the make-up done first. Plus my show coming on now and I gotta watch. After that, I'll get dressed. As a matter of fact, turn on the TV now."

This appeared on the screen: 'BREAKING NEWS! Genesis Federal Prison building has collapsed; one dead, several injured.' No one seemed quite perturbed about that newsflash.

"Oh well, guess I won't be watching my show, so crank that music 'cause it's party time!"

Getting dressed while the music was blasting, Tiana and her crew continued getting all dolled up for the major event taking place that evening. They were ready to set it off.

'You ladies ready?'

'Yes, Auntie Jay, we ready.'

'Well, let's go!' One by one, the girls proudly descended the stairs and strolled outside.

We all stood in the drive-way taking selfies and a gang load of pictures, smiling broadly, just admiring how elegant we all were as we awaited the limo to pick us up for the ride of our lives. Only problem was that the limo never showed up. Instead, this candy apple, red Mercedes CLK coupe pulled up. My niece's eyes bulged and her mouth dropped wide open. With so much screaming and laughter going on, I asked them again:

"You ladies ready?!"

'Oh my gosh, Auntie. Yes, we ready, let's go!'

Tiana hugged her mom and dad tightly and thanked them so much that we had to push her off them and hurried them into the car. As I chauffeured my niece and the girls to make their grand entrance, excitement was gushing from their eager faces. Amidst the excitement, they were trying to memorize the steps to their routine laughing and talking about who's coming and who's not. We were now on the street leading to the venue and noticed that the line was long. It seemed to be meandering around the block, appearing as though the whole neighborhood and half the city came out for this one.

'Wow!' Tiana exclaimed. 'All this for me?'

'Why not you? You're special, Baby and blessed in so many ways… this is just the beginning. Many people came out to celebrate your day.'

Tiana was ecstatic; for the first in a long time, she felt loved…wanted… she felt beautiful. Man, it couldn't get any better than this, and I hadn't even been inside yet.

'I got everything I asked for.'

'You did?'

'Well, almost everything.'

'Well, what more could you want, Young Lady?'

'A car, Auntie, but my mom and daddy said I gotta wait.'

'Oh ok. Well, just be patient and wait. Is that young man coming?'

'Who, Auntie? What young man?

'Girl, don't play; you know what young man I'm talking about….your friend from Instagram or Vine.'

'Who, Lunchtrae? Oh, I don't know, Auntie, I wish. He's famous and I have a big crush on him. He lives in Cali, not here. But, Auntie, how you know about him?'

'Oh, I thought he was someone you went to school with. Nevertheless, just get out, make your presence known and enjoy all that this night has to offer. Happy birthday Baby! Now, get ready for this grand entrance, and do it big! Let me drop the top so you girls can turn up!'

Damn I had almost spoiled the surprise. Man, the venue was amazing…pink and lavender, interspersed with cheetah print, and ignited with sparkles and diamonds everywhere. Yeah, this was Tiana's style or should I say, it was swagged out just as she had requested.

As the night progressed, the crowd grew. The girls and I were having a great time. The building was crowded; we were almost suffocating as a result the crowd density. You would have thought it was a well-advertised high profile concert or a meet-and-greet for Lunchtrae himself. His Yaga videos were all over the screen, his music was blasting over the speakers and the crowd was going wild. Just then, the music stopped.

"Attention, please. May I have your attention, please!"

Michelle began to make this long birthday speech. The lights were dimmed and the spotlight was transfixed on the birthday girl herself.

'Happy birthday to you,' someone was secretly serenading her over the intercom. The singing trailed off into an imperceptible hum. Nobody knew who it was. Then the girls burst into a melodious choir…

Happy birthday to you, happy birthday dear Tiana…

Just then, they began screaming as the spotlight moved onto the stage.

'Tiana, where you at?' the mystery voice inquired.

'I need you to come back on stage.'

As Tiana made her way back onto the stage with her mom and dad, a puzzled looked enveloped her face. The chanting cheers and screams grew increasingly louder and as she turned around to look behind her, she realized that she was being serenaded by Lunchtrae himself! She was shocked. She covered her mouth and her eyes popped out like a bush baby.

"OH MY GOODNESS! LUNCHTRAE! LUNCHTRAE!"

My niece was overwhelmed with joy.
'Lunchtrae is in the building, ya'll!' the DJ proudly announced. Tiana couldn't believe her eyes nor her ears. Her crush was in the building in her presence to help her celebrate her special day.

Tiana rushed over and gave him a mighty hug. It made her night just more memorable. The dancing, the pictures and the cake cutting were all more then we could have hoped for. The kids had a ball; so many pictures were taken that you would have thought the paparazzi were working for their next cover story for the Inquirer. The music was pulsating and irresistible, and they danced and partied until huge beads of sweat dripped from their bodies. Then the music stopped abruptly.

"Attention! Attention! May I have your attention, please?"

'What is it now?' Tiana asked.

"Tiana, I need you to come with me," Lunchtrae remarked. Tiana didn't know what was going on, and was even more surprised that she was needed outside.

Lunchtrae whispered in her ear,

'Close your eyes.' Then he gently held her by the hand and escorted her outside. She made several attempts at guessing what was up her mom and dad's sleeve now.

'Tiana, you ready for this?'

'Ready for what?'

'Your mom and dad have one more surprise for you. Are you ready?'

Just then she heard the almost soft honking of a horn. Then it grew increasingly louder, almost deafening.

She sprang to her feet, not realizing that the sound was nowhere in proximity. The screaming, cheering and excitement had overwhelmed her and as Lunchtrae whispered to her to open her eyes, he yelled,

'HAPPY BIRTHDAY from your mom and dad!' Tiana screamed and jumped delightfully. It was a car! The exact car in which she had driven to the party.

Ironically, it was actually her gift all along. Now her night was truly complete.

'Oh my gosh, I got all that I wanted, plus Lunchtrae came to my party. Ohhhh…I'm so happy! She yelled with her eyes beaming.

'I'm glad you're happy, Baby Girl. Your mom and I are so proud of you. Now, finish school and continue enjoying life as a teenager. Remember, the sky is the limit. Just remember, no dating until you're eighteen, understand?'

'Daddy!'

'No, Tiana, don't daddy me. Do you understand?'

'Yes, Daddy.'

'Good. Now, enjoy the rest of your party and drive home safely. We'll see you later. Again, Happy Birthday, Princess. We love you,' her dad reassured, beaming with unbridled pride.

As Tiana prepared to head back inside the party, I couldn't help noticing how her facial expression and mood had totally changed.

"What's wrong, Tiana? You seem a little down all of a sudden. You ok?" Lunchtrae asked.

'Yeah, I'm ok. Thank you for coming.'

'You're welcome, but are you sure you're ok?'

'You seem a little down after the conversation with your dad,' he told Tiana.

'Is it that obvious?'

'A little; you've been smiling all night and now you seem to be a little aloof.'

'Well, to be honest, it's just that my dad won't allow me to date, to talk or to socialize with boys until I'm eighteen, and it's hard. I feel like I have to sneak around just to have guy friends.'

'Well, Tiana, I don't think that's the case, but he's just being a dad. Like a lion over its cub, he wants to protect his baby. He doesn't want you to rush things or make any mistakes that you may regret. Not all men are looking for love out here. Some are angry and hate women. Just take your time, don't rush life. You never know what could happen. You might be staring love in the face. Just wait on it, and smile, it's still your night;

let's make this last hour count. You ready to go back inside now?'

'Yes, let's go.'

Tiana and Lunchtrae went back inside hand in hand to enjoy the rest of the party and the company of the partygoers. As the DJ announced the last song, Lunchtrae and Tiana took advantage of the few remaining minutes on the dance floor…they took it all in. They frolicked around, took a few more pictures, and then said their good-byes.

'I had a wonderful time, Tiana, I hope you enjoyed it as much as I did. And remember what we talked about. Just be patient and stay focused on your dreams. You'll see.' Then he gently leaned over to hug her and asked her for her phone.

"Selfie," he said, chuckling and snapped a picture of them as he kissed her on the cheek. Tiana began blushing. Finally, the party came to an end. Tiana thanked him again as they went their separate ways.

And just like that, Lunchtrae had left the building, just as he came. But the girls took the party on the road.

One by one, Tiana dropped her crew off at their different destinations. We laughed and talked about the party non-stop. It was truly a night to remember. Tiana and I pulled into the driveway and she was still talking about her night with Lunchtrae. The girl was still floating on cloud nine. We got inside the house and settled in with my brother, his wife and the other kids who were already fast asleep. Tiana was still bragging about her night.

She talked so much about the evening that I was falling asleep on her. But as long as my niece enjoyed herself, I was all for it. She went to sleep with a satisfied smile on her face with her phone still clutched in her right hand. She was protecting that cherished selfie with Lunchtrae.

Teenagers, I thought. Gotta love em.

She was finally sleeping, an indication to me that I must retire soon myself. I sat there wrestling with the thought of driving home and I realized it would be better if I just crashed on the couch. And needless to say, that is where I found rest, 'till the sun peeped in.

Chapter 4

The phone must have rung for a full two minutes before Tiana answered, 'Hello!

"Tiana, girl, oh my gosh, wake up, wake up!" The caller on the line insisted.

"What… what? I'm up, I'm up… what's wrong?"

"Girl, Lunchtrae!"

"What?!"

"Lunchtrae! He was hurt last night after the party."

"What?!"

Tiana jumped up and dashed downstairs to turn on the TV. But the news was already on….right there before the TV was Michelle and myself, appearing quite calm and somber with our eyes locked onto the screen as we heard Tiana's footsteps getting closer.

'Awe, Baby,' her mom assured, 'don't cry. He's going to be ok, he only sustained minor injuries and his manager said he's ok.'

"Can we go see him?" Tiana asked, very concerned.

"Unfortunately, no, Baby.'

"Why?"

"Because he's already out of the hospital and on a flight back to California.'

"I wish I could have said good-bye and made sure."

"He's ok, Baby. Don't worry."

"Mom, you don't understand. Lunchtrae is my friend and I don't want anything to happen to him. I'll send him a text and wait to see if he replies."

"Messages….replies?' I thought your father and I were clear on no boys until you were eighteen."

"Mom, come on now, he's different. He's a friend, but it's not like he lives here or I can talk to him or see him daily. I know what the rules are and even though I think they suck, I've listened and have been obedient so far.'

"Tiana, Baby, listen….just get some rest, don't worry. If I hear anything more, I'll let you know."

"Ok, Mom, thanks." Tiana seemed compliant but in the back of her mind, she couldn't help but to think, here is the second guy who has walked out of her life without a trace. First Big Dred, and now Lunchtrae. It didn't seem fair but life goes on.

This would be something that Tiana would learn soon enough. Tiana kept thinking about all the life lessons her dad tried to instill in her, not to mention his comment about 'boy abstinence' until she turned eighteen. She kept replaying that scene over and over until she couldn't take it anymore. She became very emotional about all the things that she thought were not fair or things that she didn't quite agree with.

"I gotta talk to him," she thought.

She was ready to have a showdown with her mom and dad.

She wanted to know why they felt that way, her dad especially. What was so bad about boys that made him put that type of stipulation on her? Besides, the neighborhood boys and those she went to school with were scared to even say hi to her because of her parents, her father especially. Both Michelle and I knew that Tiana was not going to let it go so to avoid belaboring the conversation about boys, she retreated into the kitchen and began cooking. I just tried going back to sleep. I knew that the look my niece had on her face meant it was time for the showdown. Tiana got ready to approach her mom but she thought about it. Instead, she spun around and headed back upstairs to her parents' room. From the top of the stairs she glanced over the banister at me; I knew then that it was about to happen. She took a deep breath, stepped forward and knocked on the door.

"Dad," she said calmly as she persisted with the knocking while calling her father.

'Dad.'

There was no answer. She knocked and knocked but no one ever came to the door or told her to enter. Tiana continued knocking. Then she decided to enter but with caution.

"Daddy?" She called him several times. She was getting upset because all the attempts she had made trying to get him to answer the door totally confused her. Tiana knew something wasn't right, but she got very angry when she noticed that her daddy was lying in the bed.

"Daddy!" Tiana shouted. Daddy, why are you ignoring me? I've been calling you… Daddy!" As Tiana kept calling him, she noticed he wasn't moving. He was just lying there. He was very quiet and she found this behavior very odd. Slowly she tip-toed toward the bed, and continued calling his name in a hushed tone but still, nothing. Then she inched toward the other side of the bed and carefully eased back the sheets, she stared at her dad lying there, motionless. She noticed that he didn't look the same. Then, almost involuntarily she reached out and gently touched him. He was cold.

"DADDY!!!" she wailed hysterically.

"Mom!" Her wails echoed across the rooms and we raced immediately to see wrong.

"Girl, what? Why are you screaming like you're crazy?"

Upon entering the room, we were greeted by her uncontrollable wails. Tiana was hovered over her father, pushing, pulling and shaking him, pleading with him to wake up.

"Daddy! Daddy, please Daddy! Wake up, Daddy! Mom, tell Daddy to wake up, please!'

Her mom, in a state of shock, shoved her out the way, pleading,

"Baby....Honey....please wake up!"

She was kissing and hugging him then she erupted into tears.

"Oh, Lord…oh my gosh! Lord, why? Please don't take my baby. Call 911! Hurry!"

But it was too late. We all stood there, paralyzed with fear, not wanting to think or even whisper what was obviously wrong. We were plunged into grief. I was stricken in anguish, too distraught to even mutter the inevitable. There was no pulse. No heartbeat. We didn't want to pronounce him dead…no one had the authority to do so. But from all indications, my brother was dead. I prayed he was sleeping. If only he were indeed sleeping! God had taken him. Michelle and the kids were all over him, smothering him almost, all in an attempt at waking him up. I stood there. Looking for some signs of life…none. I looked up, whispered to God, sighing, feeling numb and helpless. Tears streamed down my cheeks and soaked my tee. My brother was dead; I didn't understand.

"Why, why, why…" I lamented.

Tiana…Tiana kept flashing across my face. She placed her head on his chest and like an innocent two-year-old, she stood there, still pleading with him to wake up. Perhaps she realized that this would be the last time she would be so close to him. Reality was setting in for her first love, her best friend, her everything, her daddy. Fear and despair were etched on her tear-stained face. How could she make it without him? Her daddy was the only man in her life whom she was sure would never leave her. She thought he would always be around. As reality began to set in, Tiana's mind began to wander. Playing back all the conversations she had with her dad, she was remembering all the special moments, the life lessons he had taught her and the memories from the party, just a few hours before…. Man, none of this was making sense. What could she do? How was she going to cope without her daddy? She kept repeating these questions to herself. There were no answers. Only time would tell. With tears gushing down her cheeks, she slowly turned to me for some answers.

"Why did God have to take my daddy, Auntie?" she moaned helplessly. I wanted to know too, but I was always taught that you never questioned God. We just had to accept His plan and be strong for one another. This was shaping up to be a really hard one on us but with God, we planned to weather this storm.

The family had to band together and help Michelle and the kids bury my brother. It was one of the hardest times for the family. No one was looking forward to a funeral. I wish we could say our final goodbyes within another context, but such is the order of life. For the next couple of months, my family was on a roller coaster from hell. Tiana's attitude changed drastically, Michelle was in a state of depression and everyone was sad. Everyone was understandably seriously affected by this tragic loss because my brother played a major role in our family.

And with his passing, life in his household would never be the same.

Chapter 5

As a family, it took us many months to finally accept what had befallen us. They say time heals all wounds, only this wound was very slow in healing. Time was doing no justice in alleviating the pain and emptiness that followed. Life was returning to normal; the kids were back in school and Michelle went back to work.

Although things were shaping up a bit, Tiana was not. Things changed for the worse. She began to rebel. She was hanging out with the wrong crowd, became a truant, started smoking and drinking, and even began dating. Tiana had become loose! No dad, no respect, no rules… this seemed to be her mantra. I couldn't believe this was the same person I grew up with. Somehow I didn't know her anymore. She had, I'd say, assumed a new identity… one that was non-conforming to family rules and values. Was her rebellious behavior a cry for attention? We wanted to find out. The loss of my brother messed her up tremendously to the point where we were no longer on speaking terms. Being in her company was no longer pleasurable. She became obnoxious and her defiance and nonchalant attitude toward people who cared about her had escalated to a point where the family avoided her. This once beautiful, vibrant teen was headed for destruction, but watching her demise was not my intention. I wanted to rescue her from imminent danger, but she compelled us to love her from a distance. So, I channeled my thoughts in a different direction; I focused on loving and taking care of me. As the year passed, the healing was profound. Things looked auspicious, and the family was resolute to embrace life and happiness. But unfortunately, I was wrong. From the conversations with Michelle, she informed me (during one of my usual drop-in visits to check on the family) that my niece had completely lost her moral bearings and was going down a forbidden path.

Her level of disrespect and wonton disregard for those around her, coupled with her relentless lying and stealing, were too much for a still grieving widow to bear; hence she was thinking of doing something drastic to Tiana. She had become mean-spirited, defiant and deceptive and on several occasions, had not come home at all. My heart was in sorrow. This lifestyle that Tiana had embraced was not consistent with her upbringing. Her dad must have been turning in his grave. She was lost, but that wasn't even the worse part. The worst thing that could happen had apparently happened: Tiana was no longer pure…no longer a virgin, she was having sex. I was sick to my stomach, but the news got worse. Tiana was also pregnant! Could it get any worse? I almost gave up at that point. I wanted to kick her ass. I was incensed.

My mind flashed back on how much her daddy cherished her, all the sacrifices he made, and how he went over and beyond for her. Was that his reward?

"What an ungrateful lil' bitch!" I thought.

All I kept picturing was the TV reality show 'Sixteen and Pregnant.' Tiana let some dude trick her. No college, no degrees, no trade, no education, no marriage…but pregnant! I wanted to go find her and deal with her one on one. Oh, how I wanted to get my hands on her and beat the crap out of her! It took me a little while to calm down before I decided to have a talk with her. As I entered the neighborhood, I noticed her walking with some random dude. I thought to myself, Oh goodness, look at these two broke dummies walking and holding hands like they're in love." I honked the horn to get her attention but this mascot stood there like a deer in headlights, looking crazy. I rolled the window down to further get her attention, but she stood there for a minute or two before realizing that it was me. Upon seeing me, however, she spun around and walked the other way. I was pissed! I yelled,

"Hey, Tiana! Come here; come see me! Don't make me get out this car!"

Then, she paused and rolled her eyes and began advancing towards me. As she drew closer, I asked her where her car was and why she was walking.

"You know damn well what happened to my car!" she snapped.

"Who the hell you think you talking to?" I demanded.

She didn't utter another word. "What happened to your car and why are you walking?" I asked again.

She began to explain that her mom had taken the car from her as soon as she got wind of her despicable behavior. Her mom was even angrier when she discovered that her boyfriend was cruising around in her ride as well.

"Wow! Well, you asked for it." I chimed in indignantly.

"And just what did I ask for? What's that supposed to mean?" she inquired unashamedly.

"Just what I said, and you will not stand there and disrespect me and think that's going to fly with me!'

"Whatever!" she shrugged. "Girl, you ain't my momma, and you only a couple of years older then me, so stop acting like….."

"Oh gosh!"

"Oh, gosh, what? Why'd you say that?'

I leaned my head and looked away…

"Why are you looking like that, Ms. Willis? Why did you stop talking? Hello….Why did you say, Oh, gosh?" Dr. Maxwell asked again.

"I didn't stop talking. I just didn't let her finish her sentence."

"What do you mean?"

"I mean I got in her ass; her mouth had gotten too slick and before I knew it, I hit her; I beat her ass! Pregnant and all. But I said 'Oh gosh' because I realized I had hit a pregnant woman. And as much as it hurt me, when I thought about it, I couldn't help but to console myself because she deserved it. Doc, her mouth was too slick. I felt she needed a reality check. This lil' heifer wrote a check her butt couldn't cash.

"What does that mean?"

"Just a figure of speech, Doc, just a figure of speech."

"Well, where was her boyfriend through all of this?"

Standing there, of course, like he knew he should, but would rather not, get involved. He actually helped me put her in the car. He did the right thing or I would have smacked his ass too!'

"Wait…put her in the car? What happened…
why?"

Yes, Doc, the car. I knocked her butt out, and I couldn't leave her on the pavement. Her boyfriend just patted her face with some water and allowed her to sleep.

And as she slept on the back seat, he and I had an interesting conversation. And from what he said, the pregnancy 'just happened.' Well, that's according to him; they weren't trying but he loved and wanted to be with her and to be there for the baby. Also, he wasn't completely aware of the situation, so he tried his best to reassure me that his love for her was genuine. After about ten minutes or so, Tiana came around; she woke up still talking crap. I asked her boyfriend to give us a minute and he complied. I was beginning to realize that this conversation was going nowhere, so I stopped trying to talk because she was not making any sense and I was getting angry all over again.

She was worse than I had thought; I started to think that there was no hope for her and I hated to see this girl like this. But I guess I had no choice but to surrender. If it weren't for the baby she was carrying, I swear, you would have thought she was on drugs. And as I threw her dumbass out of my car, I began to get misty-eyed, I just stared at her and the tears swelled in my eyes. I drove off blinded by tears, knowing that this would be the last time I would try to reach out to my niece for a very long time.

"Enough about her, for a minute."

The doctor stretched a bit and yawned; I hoped I was not boring him but he assured me that the events were intriguing and encouraged me to continue.

"So, let's get back to Mr. Derric, I mean, the invincible Mr. Big Dred."

Chapter 6

As Big Dred opened his eyes, he realized that he was in a strange place strapped down to a stretcher once again. "Where am I? What happened? Agghhh… my head, my arms. What's going on?"

"Hello again, Mr. Patson, how do you feel?"

"I'm in pain, ma'am. What happened to me?"

"Well,' the nurse explained, 'all I was told was that you were trapped under some heavy debris and rubbish, is that right?"

"Debris and what?" "The building collapsed and you were trapped under the trash and stuff. You were out for a minute before they found you. But thank God, you are alive."

"Barely, man, I seem to have pure bad luck. I've only been in prison a year and a few months and it seems like this hospital is more of my cell than the actual one at the institution. I've been between Medical and the hospital several times; believe me, I'm tired. I'll be so glad when this bid is over this time. I promise I ain't ever going back.' He tried to convince himself.

"Well, at least when it's over for you this time, you will have something to look forward to."

"What do you mean?" he snapped.

"Excuse me, I've said too much." She caught herself.

"Just know you've got a major blessing coming your way dealing with this brush with death."

"Ok, whatever that means."

"Just get better and you'll see."

As Big Dred lay there looking at the ceiling, he began daydreaming. Thinking about all that had taken place in his life and why it was happening to him. 'What is going on with me man…. why me? Why am I going through all this hell? I really need my momma,' he murmured.

He was heartbroken. He was enveloped with emptiness and a feeling of loneliness as there seemed to be no one in his corner. He wanted to talk to his mom so badly…

"Nurse!" Big Dred shouted.

"When will I be able to use the phone? I need to make a call."

"Use the phone? Mr. Patson, you know that's not possible,' she said sarcastically.

"Phone calls for you in here are prohibited, all you can do is rest. Just rest. I'm sure your family is aware of the situation and will be updated as progress is made."

Big Dred stayed in the hospital for the next month as a result of the injuries he sustained. Then back to business as usual, back to the institution he went. This time he had nothing on his mind but getting the opportunity to talk to his momma.

After a few months of not being able to use the phone, Big Dred finally got his chance.

"Hello, you have a collect call." His mother quickly answered the nagging ringing. His mother didn't hesitate to accept the call; you could hear the excitement in her voice from a mile away.

"Hey, Baby!"

"Hey, Ma! What's up? What's going on?"

"Nothing. Why haven't you called? It's been almost three months since we last spoke."

"Momma, it's been so much going on here; you just don't know."

"You want to talk about it, son?"

"No, not really, Momma; I'm just ready to come home. I'm tired of this place already. I just got out of the hospital."

"What! What happened, baby?" "Well, the unit that I'm housed in collapsed on me."

"What? That was you on the news?" "

The news?" "Yeah, a couple of months ago that institution was on the news for that very reason. I tried to contact your counselor to find out what was going on with you, but they wouldn't put me through.'

"Well then, yes, that was me."

"My goodness, baby, I saw that and when they mentioned the name of the institution, it made me nervous. I kept watching it. Somebody got killed in that accident, too!'

"What! Really, Momma? I didn't know that," Big Dred said, surprised.

"Thank God you're ok, son." With just one minute remaining, they hurried the conversation.

"Man, that couldn't have been fifteen minutes?"

"Don't worry about it baby, just call back."

"It's ok, Momma, I'll call back tomorrow. But wait, Ma, do me a favor. I need you to try and find somebody for me."

"Who?"

"Her name is Tiana."

"You talking about that hot fast-tale gal up the road?"

"She... 'Hot' Momma?"

"Well, wait, let me take that back because I don't know; I'm not gone judge her. I just see her walking up and down the streets every day, but don't worry I'll see what I can do, son. When you gone call back?"

"In a few days. Love you Momma."

"Love you too baby."

Now as you know, Big Dred was serving a three-year bid, so he had a lot of time to think. His normal activities became daily routines and the phone calls home to his mom were all the same. He'd call and ask about her health, his kids and if she found out any news on Tiana.

But it was never any luck. It was always the same old thing. But in actuality, she just didn't have the heart to tell her son that Tiana was not thinking about him. She was living her life and pregnant with someone else's child. As a mother, she didn't want to break his heart, so she kept it from him. His mom kept telling him she hadn't seen her despite the fact that Tiana would walk by her house every day with a piece of stick in her hand, occasionally kicking a few loose rocks along the sidewalk. She hated to deceive him but at the same time, it was for his own good. She was trying to save her son from some serious heartbreak. She had witnessed how he had suffered at the hands of other females, and she didn't want him to have to go through all of that stress again.

One afternoon as Big Dred and his mom were having their weekly conversation, there was an unexpected interruption, a constant loud message over the intercom. The message was followed by some names but Big Dred didn't pay it any mind. The interruption was becoming annoying because it was very loud. It played two more times and a fellow inmate started yelling upon realizing that it was his name being called.

Big Dred's name was being called repeatedly over the intercom. His mom even heard the guy yelling at him for not answering the page.

"Why they calling you, Derric?"

"I don't know, Momma. But don't worry, Ma, I'll call you back. Let me go see what they want with me. Love you."

"Love you too, baby."

After hanging up the phone with his momma, he went to investigate.

"Inmate Patson, Inmate Derric Patson!" the officer yelled.

"Yeah, I'm here!"

"You can't hear? Dude, they've been calling you for a minute now. You're needed in Mrs. Cameron's office."

"Counselor's Cameron's office? Not again."

"Man, just head down to her office and see what's going on,' he was firmly advised. And off he went, nervously hurrying down to his counselor's office. When Big Dred arrived there, he realized he wasn't alone. He thought to himself, "Damn, what now? Why are all these people in here and what the hell happened now?"

"Mr. Patson! We've been waiting on you," Counselor Cameron remarked.

"You've been waiting on me? I thought I was in the wrong place. What's up?" Big Dred exclaimed sarcastically.

"Come on in, have a seat. Why would you think you're in the wrong place?"

"I don't know… all these people in here for one thing."

"Well actually, all these people are here for you."

"For me? Why?" "Yes, let me explain."

"Let you explain…? Listen, ma'am, no disrespect but I don't want no more meetings and I can't stand anymore bad news. Besides, what kind of meeting is this involving the warden and whoever else these people are?"

"Mr. Patson, please sir, just have a seat. I know you're wondering why you're here. Well, these gentlemen and Warden Jacob are here due to the incident that took place several months ago."

"What about it?"

"Well, Mr. Patson. I'll take it from here." The warden insisted.

"Mr. Patson, these gentlemen are from the legal department and they work here at the prison. They have been a part of the team that was investigating the incident that took place when the Medical Southeast Housing unit collapsed with you still inside. And during that investigation, they came to the conclusion that there was no way you could have been aware of, caused or even attempted any of your injuries that you sustained. Therefore you are entitled to some compensation."

"Compensation?" Big Dred inquired.

"Yes, Mr. Patson, you heard right, Compensation."

"But, what kind of compensation are we talking about though?"

"Compensation for pain and suffering. Are you still with me so far?"

"Shit, hell yeah, more than ever now! Keep talking."

"Wait. Right now we have an amount but it has to be split equally because of the other parties involved."

"How many parties are involved?"

"There were three in total, but one passed away and the other one has been relocated to another facility due to the nature of his injuries.

I also need you to know that this is a process; it will take sometime to get the case closed out. All the paperwork has to be processed to payout the medical bills and other expenses."

"What expenses? Hell, I'm already in prison."

"True but…. Mr. Patson, any way it goes, you will be well compensated regardless. We just have to close out the investigation."

"So, why are you telling me all this now, then?"

"Because it's part of the process, and the other reason we are telling you now is because there is a good chance that you may make it home before you see any money."

"So, how do I know what's what? What will I receive?"

"I don't know just yet, but you will receive an equal portion. Just continue to go to the therapy sessions, document everything and we'll be in touch."

"Therapy? What therapy? Now, how am I supposed to document and keep tabs on all these things?" Big Dred quizzed him.

"You want your money, right?"

"Hell yeah; excuse me… yes, sir, I want my money."

"Well, you'll make it happen. By the way, here's a tablet; just keep up with everything you can and we'll be in touch. I also need you to know that you have to be patient and keep this to yourself unless you want a lot of new friends and problems to go along with it. Can you handle that, Mr. Patson?"

"Oh yeah, no doubt. I mean, no problem, sir."

"Anything else, Mrs. Cameron?" Warden Jacob asked.

"No, sir."

"Well, Mr. Patson, you can head back to your dorm now." They all arose, shook hands and parted ways.

"Thank you, sir. Thank you, Mrs. Cameron."

Now for the first time throughout Big Dred's bid, he seemed happy. He left out of that meeting with his head held high, chest poked out, and feeling like he was THE MAN. He headed back to his room with the thoughts of being financially set and not having any worries when this money finally came through. He would be the man again. No worries, mom and the kids would be set and he could sit back and enjoy life. This would the motivation he needed. And for the next two years, this would become his main focus. He stayed motivated and took care of himself by taking his daily meds, exercising regularly, eating right and keeping his eye on all the latest cars and fashion he could think of. He had a plan. Visits and communication with his mom and the kids couldn't be better. Time was flying and he was a man on a mission. A man with a plan who didn't have a care in this world but to get out of bondage. With this new found financial freedom ahead, he couldn't help but think of being able to get back at everyone who had turned their backs on him. And his plan would be set in motion just as soon as those gates were opened for his release.

Chapter 7

Now for the next few years, Ms. Tiana was catching hell. Life was already taking its toll on her, but she tried very hard to suppress her emotions and camouflage her suffering. She had given birth and time was flying by. She was also dating someone she was no longer in love with; someone she didn't even have feelings for anymore. The love was gone, but she tried her best to make it work for the sake of my new nephew Chase. Who, by the way, was getting so big and just about ready to celebrate his first birthday a few months later. Tiana had already begun planning the baby's birthday party or should I say, the one-year-old's birthday bash. She wanted everyone to be a part of this grand celebration. I guess she was indirectly trying to impress everybody, her mom in particular; she just really wanted to let her see how 'good' life was and how well she was handling and enjoying her new found motherhood status. Well I, for one, wasn't impressed. Because soon, it would all fall apart. Since her once boyfriend, now baby-daddy, was not working and was living off of her, she could barely keep a dime. The struggle was definitely real. They fought and argued all the time.

"Excuse me, Ms. Willis, if you and your niece weren't on speaking terms, how on earth did you know what was going on with her?" The doctor asked with grave concern.

"Dr. Maxwell, really? One thing that will never change is who she is to me; she will always be my niece. I kept my concerns strictly on her and the well-being of my nephew Chase. And although I didn't agree with her decisions and the poor choices she had made, when all is said and done, she's blood, she's my family.

"Ok, I understand, continue."

"Well any who, as I was saying…."

They weren't getting along. She wanted to give up but she'd rather fake it than look like a failure. So she attempted to stick it out. But after all the broken promises, constant arguments, struggles and disappointments, she was slowly giving up. This was

Tiana's breaking point but the final straw was the cheating. Tiana had caught her man with another female in the bed that they shared. That was the defining moment; she lost it. Overcome by untamed fury.... she attacked the female, ripped her hair, slapped her around several times and beat her so badly that she needed medical attention. Then, she turned on him and unleashed a few slaps to him, too, but that jerk tried to run. He was so scared, he sprinted towards the bathroom which pissed her off even more. He was dodging objects of all shapes and sizes that were being hurled at him... anything in arm's reach from the comb, the kettle to the cell phone, a few missing his head by an inch.

Well me? Sorry, oh no! I wouldn't have missed for anything.... that head would have been completely severed! But she's not me, and I'm not her. She let him get away. Well, not really, because the coward only made it into the bathroom where he locked himself inside. Tiana almost caught a case behind all that foolishness. And although she was in a rage, she felt bad for beating the girl like she did, so she immediately called the paramedics for her but not before she cleaned house. Tiana went crazy throwing out clothes and shoes, busting up the TVs and breaking and tossing out furniture. It was a nightmare indeed. She was so furious in all the commotion that she was totally oblivious of the police officer standing in the doorway.

"Ma'am, ma'am, ma'am!" the police yelled.

"What!" she replied.

"What's going on here? You wanna come outside and tell us what's going on?"

"Hell no, this is my house. And who the hell called y'all anyway? You better get that bitch off the floor and that muthafucka that's locked in the bathroom and ask them what happened."

"No, we wanna talk to you."

"Well, officer, I don't have anything to say, I only hope the bitch makes it.' Tiana was being disrespectful in her anger.

'She let that muthafucka trick her into coming into my house and fucking in my bed!"

"Whoa, wait. I thought this was a domestic dispute?" inquired the officer.

"A domestic dispute? Ain't no domestic dispute. I don't know that bitch and he knows he shouldn't have had her in here 'cause he wouldn't be locked in the bathroom. He should not have let her in my house."

The police couldn't help but laugh. He shook his head and warned Tiana that she'd better hope that the girl didn't press charges or she'd be going straight to jail.

Why did they say that? By then, a small, controlled crowd had gathered outside as soon as the paramedics pulled up.

Tiana slipped back into the house and dashed straight for the bathroom.

"Hey, ma'am,' the officer said cautiously. "You can't go in there!"

"My house? I can't go into my house?" yelled Tiana.

"Well, I tell you what. You can get ready to read me my rights 'cause I'm going back in to finish what I started since I'm already going to jail. If that hoe decides to press charges after I caught her in MY bed in MY house with MY man, she'd better be prepared for another ass-whopping. I did her a favor by calling the paramedics because I didn't have to. By the way…who called the police?"

"Ma'am, I don't know. But we were notified when the paramedics were called. It's just procedure."

"No, it's not, you're lying!" she yelled accusingly.

"Ma'am, don't tell me. And don't tell us how to do our job. I'm warning you."

"You're warning me?"

"Yes, I'm warning you. Now I understand you're upset and all but there is a proper way of handling this situation. You're angry, someone's locked inside the bathroom and there is someone lying here on the floor, crying and in pain.

But I do understand your point. Now, we have to see what's going on from the other two people involved. So follow me back outside to the patrol car and wait until the paramedics and I both are done with helping this young lady and the investigation."

"Well, can I at least get my baby?"

"Baby? You have a baby?"

"Yes, inside the house!"

"You mean to tell me a baby slept through all of this commotion?" "

I guess so."

"Well, stay right here; I'll get the baby. Don't you move! As a matter of fact, sit here in the back of the car."

Surprisingly, Tiana did as she was told without arguing and hopped into the back of the police car. The officer then squeezed himself into the apartment and within seconds, he emerged, clutching my nephew in his arms and handed him to his mother while she sat there patiently watching the police and paramedics do their job. After a two-hour wait, they finally came back to the car to talk to Tiana.

"Tiana, ok, here's the deal," the officer said. 'I'm going to let you go, but I must tell you this: Don't go looking for no more trouble."

"Well, where is he going?"

"Tiana…let me finish. He's going to be escorted off the property and then you will be allowed to go back in. I'd advise you to go down to the police department tomorrow and file an injunction 'cause I'm almost certain he'll be back."

"Well, if you know he'll be back why won't you arrest him now?" Tiana asked the officer.

"Because if I arrest him, you're going, too. See where I'm going with this?"

"Yes, sir," she quickly responded.

"Ok, so, sit tight, we're waiting on his ride and for him to get his things, well his clothes, then he's out of here! Ok?"

"Ok."

After another twenty-minute wait, the smoke cleared and he was gone. Tiana was allowed back inside the house. She paced up and down, examining the damage and the mess that she had intentionally caused.

'Dammmmn!' she mumbled, "A tornado ripped through this shit!"

At that point, she grew more confused as she sauntered through the apartment. She did one logical thing though, she called her mom.

Calling Michelle was the best decision she could have ever made. For the first time in a long time, she humbled herself, poured her heart out, and pleaded for herself and the baby to return home. It seemed like the lost sheep was finally finding its way home."

"Come back home?" the doctor asked.

"Yes, Dr. Maxwell, she asked to come back. But not before some new rules and guidelines were given. You see, Tiana didn't quite care about that apartment anyway; hell it wasn't in her name. She had messed up badly, her mom and dad had tried desperately to prevent her from making the same mistakes they made when they became teen parents, but she wouldn't listen. She knew that if she were to return home, it was going to be by her mom's rules and her rules only. We all were relieved that she had finally come to her senses and things were going to be great as soon as she moved back home. Well that's just an optimistic thought. And for a while, things were looking good. Both she and the baby had settled in beautifully: she was doing great and had even earned her car back. Going to school, learning to communicate with the family better and taking care of my nephew was more than one could ask for. But as time went by, it became clear that all was not well. She was still unhappy, very unhappy. Being back home meant that her mom would monitor her every move, and guys wouldn't be able to come and go as they pleased. It was back to having rules, just not Tiana's rules.

Now, the mere thought of answering to someone else just wasn't sitting too well with her and with a baby in the picture, she considered herself a grown ass woman; therefore, she wasn't embracing that too graciously. So her initial excitement soon faded as she began to realize that she didn't want to be back at the house with her mom. Well, she had no choice at the time but to go with the flow and just suck it up for that moment. What else was she going to do?

Not that she had options anyway. As time progressed, she was determined to get back on her own but she knew it wouldn't be easy. She had bitten off far more than she could chew... trying to take care of Chase, going back to school and dealing with the new rules of the house were overwhelming and had undoubtedly thrown her in a state of frustration. She became mean, cold and distanced from family members. Then, she developed the habit of leaving the baby with people indiscriminately, just to avoid his constant crying and having to deal with him, I remember Michelle calling me one night about a particularly disturbing incident. It was a dark, cold night when Tiana took the baby for a walk. The strangest and most sickening thing happened that, to date, has left everyone baffled and questioning her mental state. This girl left her innocent, defenseless baby outside in the cold right at the doorsteps so that she didn't have to hear him cry, and she just walked away. This was when my sister-in-law began noticing the unexpected changes in her again. Every time he would cry, it was something different.

She was out of control. But he was still her baby. Michelle made sure she didn't abuse or hurt him, but she wanted her to learn that she was responsible for this precious life and that she could not take her baby for granted. My niece loved attention, and that's what she was looking for. Also, Tiana's mood swings were always roller-coastering; she was so unpredictable and you never knew who you were dealing with especially after the terrible break-up between her and the baby daddy. Post–partum, I guess, but she wasn't handling any of these post-birth situations well at all. She was an inconsiderate bitch! She was consumed with animosity and frustration, and the poor harmless infant was at the receiving end… the recipient of all this vicious anger!

There was another time, too, when Tiana was out strolling the baby and he became very cranky, crying and throwing an uncontrollable fit. The first thing any sensible mother would have done is to seek out the cause of the baby's discomfort. Well, not so with this miserable lil' bitch. She sprang into a rage and started yelling at the poor child. Her shouts were audible enough for the neighbors and passers-by to get on her case. Now, you would think that out of embarrassment, this girl would at least tone down or stop her wicked behavior toward the poor baby. Some people shouted at her, others cursed, a few were offering some advice and the rest stood by in disbelief. One kind, middle-aged lady actually hurried over, unfastened his straps and snatched poor Chase from the stroller; guess this was another attempt at soothing the baby but unfortunately, it didn't help. And would you believe that she still continued along the path with the baby crying? Then as she was passing what appeared to be a quaint looking two-story house, she noticed an elderly lady swinging in a dark-stained antique hammock beneath a big tree that had provided enough shade for the neighborhood. In a kind voice, the lady asked,

'What's wrong with the baby, dear?"

"I don't know, ma'am, but God knows; I wish he'd stop! I wish he'd just shut up… Damn!"

"Oh no, don't you ever let me see you do that again. This is a baby, a helpless child; you spread those legs and brought him into this world!"

"But he won't stop crying. What am I supposed to do, ma'am?"

"So? Hell, you were a baby once, too. Bring him here!" As Tiana began walking towards this caring stranger, the woman immediately realized who she was and exclaimed,

"Tiana, is that you?"

"Yes, Mrs. Clark, it's me! How you doing?"

"I'm doing fine, honey, besides you hollering at this poor baby. How you? You know I've been looking for you."

"Really? Why you looking for me?"

"Well, I was really just trying to get a message to you." And just as the conversation was about to kick off, Mrs. Clark's phone rang. "

What time is it?" she asked.

"Seven thirty-five."

"Oh my goodness, hold on a minute, honey. I gotta get this call! Don't you go nowhere!"

"Ok, I won't."

And with a distanced countenance, Tiana stood there waiting.

"Well, hey there, I was sitting outside talking to this young lady," Mrs. Clark said to the caller.

Tiana didn't know what was going on and she was tired of waiting; she was ready to go but as she was waiting, she overheard Mrs. Clark telling the caller that she was standing right in front of her. Totally dumbfounded, Tiana didn't know who could possibly want to speak to her or who even knew she was at this strange lady's house. She wondered.

"Excuse me, Mrs. Clark, I don't mean to be rude," she said.

"I'm going to get ready to go home now."

"Hold on a minute; just a second." Mrs. Clark said.

'Someone wants to speak to you." As she handed Tiana the phone, she smiled. "Hello?" Tiana said.

"Hello Beautiful, what's up? How you been?"

"Who is this?"

"You don't know? Really? I know it's been a minute but damn, that's messed up. You forgot about me?"

"I'm sorry, but I'm lost."

"Don't be… this is Derric."

"Who?"

"Tiana? Man, for real… for real? This is Big Dred!"

"OMG! Really? Heeeey! I'm so sorry. It's been a few years."

"Yes, I know, but I been looking for you. What you doing at my ol' lady's house?"

"Yo' ol' lady?"

"Yeah, my momma."

"I didn't know Mrs. Clark was your mom. Wow, small world."

"Why you shocked?"

"Just didn't know that she was your mom. It's not like I've been around your family to know."

"Well, we're going to have to change that just as soon as I get home."

The conversation went on and on for a few more minutes before the infamous minute warning recording interrupted the conversation. The phone call was about to end. Tiana and Big Dred had already made big plans to continue this long overdue conversation at a later date.

"So, when can I hit you up again? Where are you headed?" he asked.

"Home, I was out walking my baby when your mom stopped me."

"A baby? You got a baby on me? Man, damn, I didn't know that. So you got a man?"

"No, I don't have a man anymore. We're not together. I'm single. A single mother."

"Ah man, sorry to hear that. But check this out... I want to talk to you. When can you come back to my mom's house?"

"Whenever you need me to."

"Oh yeah, like that?"

"Yep, just like that. Just let your mom know and she'll tell me."

"Shit, I'm telling you now. I'll call tomorrow at six o' clock so be there."

"Ok, I will." As the call disconnected, Mrs. Clark smiled broadly and began her commentary.

"Man, you didn't even give me a chance to say good night. What did he say?"

"Well, basically, he wants me to come back over tomorrow and he's going to call at six o' clock."

"So I guess you coming over tomorrow at six. And bring that baby; don't you leave him home."

"Ok, I will. So I guess I'll see you then. Have a good night."

Chapter 8

Tiana's walk home never felt better. She was stepping on air; the gaiety in her steps was an indication of a taste of happiness and perhaps, bright hopes for the future. This was a feeling she had not experienced in a long time, especially since Chase's birth. Tiana was finally happy. The anger and misery on her face had all disappeared since that short conversation just a few minutes before. Pleasant thoughts raced through her mind over and over, playing back all those moments she and Big Dred had shared.

She couldn't wait until six o' clock the following day. She was ready to let go and embrace the new life that seemed apparent in the near future… oh, she wished. Her knight in shining armor had resurfaced! She was planning to get to his mom's house early so she would be there when he called and she could get a break from the baby since Mrs. Clark had insisted that he accompany her. Tiana was daydreaming like crazy. Her mind was racing… her heart was doing the talking now and her emotions were driving her mad. This time, it seemed like she was willing to take chances…there was no stopping her. She knew that Big Dred liked her even though there was a six-year age difference, and she fervently prayed that this time around would be it. She was bent on seizing the moment at whatever cost necessary. She didn't see herself as that same little girl who had been crushing on an older man. And she hoped he could see that, too. Man, with so many thoughts flooding her little brain, she was confused. And from all accounts, she was basking in her moment so much that you couldn't tell her anything! The revelation was fast approaching and everyone would see. It was indeed a euphoric moment. She was at Mrs. Clark's home, or it maybe more appropriate to say, Big Dred's house… waiting, impatient and excited. Then she took a deep breath and whispered to herself, "The moment is here; finally, my baby is finally getting ready to call."

"The low-life had her hooked already."

"Low-life? Wait, why did you call him a low life?" the doctor asked.

"Because in my eyes, he was and still is.' He was more than that, but I can't call him what I really want to call him."

Of course, I really don't think Mrs. Clark would find these remarks flattering and would have obviously been quite offended by my insensitive comments concerning her son. But these are my thoughts Doc."

"Ok, sorry, Ms. Willis; continue."

"Well, the day went on as planned. She got there early and sat patiently waiting until he called. And bingo! The ringing of the phone was like heavenly music to Tiana's ears because she was certain that this was the call! Not even a minute after the clock had struck six, it was six o' clock on the dot. Mrs. Clark answered while Tiana sat there, nervous, hands sweating and her heart losing its rhythm. And with a brief hello to his momma, he and Tiana lost no time and began their long overdue conversation. Man, this dude was good. He sold my poor naïve niece all kinds of fancy, lofty dreams; he told her all the things he thought she wanted and needed to hear. She couldn't wait for him to come home."

"She couldn't wait after having just one conversation with him?" the doctor asked.

"Doc, her head was so messed up about this dude again. She was already talking about them moving in with his momma just to be close to him.

The phone calls had become very frequent and they were driving her crazy.'

"Wow, he was good."

"Ya think?"

It was ridiculous. But that's when she really started rebelling again. She resorted to her old, dirty ways... secretive, leaving Chase with her younger siblings to go to his mom's to talk to him or just trying to hide the fact all the way around that she was conversing with this man.

She even bought a cell phone just so he didn't have to call the house. Then she took it even further: she was lying about school just to try and go to visit this man, but she had no luck since she had yet to be approved as a visitor. And when my sister-in-law would ask her what she was up to, Tiana would have selective memory, only telling what she wanted her to know. But, who did she think she was fooling? Essentially, that was our question. Everybody knew there was someone new in her life, we just didn't know who. My sister-in-law was very worried about her, but she realized quickly that Tiana would have to hit rock bottom to understand that she couldn't hide certain things from certain people. I was on the phone one afternoon when she made another desperate attempt at starting a conversation with Tiana, but she didn't want to have anything to do with that discussion. Needless to say, I was pissed; however, I tried really hard to keep out of it this time. I was kind of allowing her mother to take charge of this situation; I didn't want to be too intrusive. But the last thing I remember my sister-in-law saying to her, and I'll never forget it, was...

"Everything that glitters ain't gold. You better be careful of the company you keep. 'Cause what's done in the dark will always come to light somehow, someday."

Immediately, Tiana went irate and started screaming and shouting, "You just don't want me to be happy! You trying to jinx me. You wish for me to be alone, miserable and unhappy like you! Leave me alone!

Y'all don't ever wish me good luck! Just always negative!"

We knew right away that there was no getting through to her. She was impenetrable! We all would have to just sit back and watch her play Russian roulette with her life. It was unfathomable to even imagine that one young person could be so cold, calculated and defiant. She was bound to meet her doomsday if she didn't change.

It was hard but what could we do? She stopped speaking to her mom and began running with some chicks she had befriended while in school. Not to mention when her friends came home from college, they would all hang out together. But Tiana let loose when she was finally given the approval to start visiting this dude.

He introduced her to other inmate girlfriends who in return, introduced her to a whole new world: prison life. And she was riding high and enjoying every minute of it! This went on for about a year; the more she ran the streets, the closer she became to his mother and his kids.

She was definitely in love again and desperate to be with this 'mystery man.'

"Why did you call him a 'mystery man'?" the doctor asked, appearing exhausted but still listening.

"Because at that particular time, that's exactly what he was…. a puzzle. I didn't know him. My sister-in-law Michelle didn't know him or his family either, so he was truly a mystery to all of us."

"Hmmm, continue."

"What's the 'hmmm' about, Doc?"

"No reason, just taking notes. Continue."

"Well, like I was saying, this guy was nothing more than a big riddle that was difficult for us to figure out.

Things were becoming more difficult for us to deal with as time went on. Especially when Michelle moved out of the house that she once shared with my deceased brother and raised their children in."

"Why did she move?"

"She wanted to downsize… too many memories and she said it was too big for her and my nephews.

Remember, there were still two more kids under Tiana. And Michelle just really wanted to close that chapter of their lives since my brother died there. It had proven to be too much for her."

Chapter 9

This was music to Tiana's ears, knowing that her mom was moving would give her the perfect opportunity to get her another place of her own. This was ideal for her and her many friends since they all spent so much time together. She was out to impress and make a point; hence, she desperately wanted to try it on her own first. And remember now, she was preparing for the dude's grand homecoming. So being on her own would make it that much easier, especially since it was less than six months away. All she could think about was not having to listen to all the nagging, watching over her shoulder, people telling her what to do, and she could come and go as she pleased. Just the thought had her in hog heaven. So, she immediately braced herself and started a frantic house search.

She walked along the avenues every day, searching for a place to rent. She peeped into every crevice until she found the perfect spot. It was hard but after weeks of searching, she finally found somewhere in a very nice upscale area. It had everything she was yearning for and more. The only problem was that it was out of her price range… she was tilting her hat where she couldn't reach it… in an attempt at living above her means without even a steady income. Consequently, she had no choice but to find a roommate. Well, with a hefty rent, utilities and maintenance… that was no slice of cake! So this warranted three roommates to make ends meet. It was survival time! I still don't know whose name the apartment or house was in because Tiana had no job. She had lost her job because her mystery man became a priority. All she had was the money from school and the lump sum from her dad's death; but still, that didn't stop her. She desperately wanted to make that apartment or house a home. And when I heard about it, I felt it was impossible… impossible for four young women and a baby to make a house a home. She was headed for disaster, but we had to let her live her life, allow her to make her own mistakes and learn the hard way. She wasn't hearing us anyway, but we thought it was worth trying. All we knew is that Tiana had a man in her life that she was crazy about and there was no stopping her. She was totally consumed by him that nothing else mattered then, not even the welfare of her own child. She totally forgot about that lil' dude from her past, the baby-daddy to be exact.

Her mind was on the dude but every now and then, she still found the time to text or talk to Lunchtrae. They still talked occasionally but that man wasn't thinking about her; he was getting his money and living. Not to mention that if he knew what she had going on, those conversations wouldn't take place either. He actually did turn out to be a real good friend to Tiana, but she couldn't see it. Tiana instantly became a 'prison wife' and any other dude who was interested in her they no longer had a chance. So, she stuck to her daily routine: running to prison for visitation, the gym, and school whenever she was in the mood to attend. She was determined to get ready for this man. She even started purchasing clothes and shoes for him, lingerie for herself, and sex toys and shit. Where all this money came from was the biggest puzzle; nevertheless, this lil' trick found it! Fascinated by the strangest B.S., I couldn't believe the shit I was hearing on the street about my niece. And in my eyes, she badly wanted to be a wife. I was simply frustrated by the fact that she wanted to start a life with a man she knew nothing about. She was a kid when he left, shit she was still a kid for all I cared; a kid making dumb ass decisions... one after the other.

"Why do you feel like she didn't know him?" the doctor asked.

"Hell, she didn't; she was in love with an image, a vision of what she saw on TV and what her mom and dad once had. But I was always taught to be careful what you wish for because you just might get it."

"You're so right, so right,' he again interjected.

"I'm taken aback by all of this, she was one busy young woman, it seems."

Now with all that my niece had going on at that point... going to school, running up and down the road for visitation, the homecoming of her man, taking care of my nephew and learning how to cook... I was in shock. It made me wonder where she was getting all this energy from and why she was going through all this to impress this clown. And watch this... while Tiana was out there playing 'Susie homemaker,' Mr. Big Man was being Mr. Calm, Cool and Collected. He became more focused on his appearance because he wanted to make sure he was the man again. So when he stepped out, everybody would know that 'The Man' was back on the scene.

He worked out morning, noon and night, religiously, to acquire and maintain his ideal image of a centerfold that would make a bitch wiggle and wet on sight. And I can't lie, he did just that. When I finally saw him, I was like "Damn!" That dude was something serious for real.

Anyways in prison, he even started reading more. From biblical narratives to recipes, newspaper articles and editorials, to pass the time, I guess; nevertheless, that was commendable. One afternoon, he happened to read a brochure that plunged him into deep thoughts. It was a brochure titled, "Men and their Prostate." It was very profound. 'Staying healthy, staying active and staying fit. Get an Exam.' He pondered on that one seriously for a while then he gradually grew nervous; but he thought long and hard before tossing it to the side. But even then, it stayed on his mind. He wondered if he should go and sign up for this procedure, only something kept holding him back. He decided that he would pray about it and make his decision after visitation with his mom and Tiana the following day.

He wanted to make sure that his visit was a favorable one, so he deliberately dismissed the idea altogether and just went to bed. As the sun began to rise and the alarm sounded, Big Dred got up and started with his daily routine. He was excited because it was that time again: time for the first of his three weekly visits with Tiana. He worked out, ran the track a bit, had his breakfast and then took a shower all before she arrived.

He sat on his bed waiting patiently for his name to be called over the intercom. And as usual, Tiana showed up for visitation and things went just as planned… no worries and not a care in the world. They kicked back, threw caution to the wind, and it was just him and his boo, making plans for his grand comeback. Dude was ready for the world! They laughed and talked about everything: the past, the present, their future… their wants and needs from one another.

Even a blind man could see that Tiana was in love, deeply in love… or so, it appeared. Their conversations were as intimate as the environment allowed, but they took it to a whole new level.

He was almost making love, only it was to her mind. By the end of visitation and the intercom announcements, Big Dred knew, finally, that this girl was special. That kiss they shared before walking out sealed the deal; he knew he had her. He gently pulled her closer to him and their mouths locked in a deep, passionate kiss. He was in a trance as he sucked on her tongue and playfully nibbled her lips. By then, their public affectionate display was like a movie scene; they had captured the attention of a few inmates and visitors who stood in awe, some admiring while others were obviously repulsed by their behavior. There's no doubt that the security guard himself was enjoying the scene but he came across, however, to pry them apart, yelling,

"Patson! Damn break it up! Get a room!"

Big Dred spun around, very annoyed, backed off, sighed, shook his head in frustration, and reluctantly retreated to the entrance to be escorted to his cell. Tiana stood in line waiting to be ushered from the building. As Big Dred proceeded to his cell, the idea hit him to walk by the medical facility to set up an appointment for a prostate exam but he hesitated. The process haunted him and he was about to change his mind but he was aware of the importance of this examination because he didn't want to run the risk of being another casualty. He entered the medical unit and headed straight to the counter where he was greeted by a nurse.

"Hello, how can I help you?"

"Sup! Yeah, I need to make an appointment for my prostate exam."

"Ok, gimme a second. What's your inmate number?"

She started entering the numbers as he recited, "55569-1-2-3."

"Name?"

"Derric Patson."

"Ok, well… hmm, hold on a second."

"What? Wait… why…. what now?"

"Nothing, Patson, I just have to get the right forms. Since it looks like you're eligible for your pre-release physical next month, I'm going to put in the request and note that you want your prostate exam done, too. How does that sound?"

"It's cool, I guess. I just want to get all this done and over with."

"Well, you should be happy; you're almost out of here. Go ahead and sign the consent form for treatment and we'll send you out a reminder in a few days to a week before your scheduled physical and procedure is set to take place.

"Ok, cool. Thanks," he replied. He left the medical unit and returned to his room. At that point, it really hit him; it was almost time for his release… a long awaited one. His three-year bid was almost over and he was ready for his comeback. He couldn't wait to tell the good news to his momma and Tiana. His excitement had by then reached fever pitch but he restrained himself from spilling too much, lest there's a twist of events; so he decided to wait until the time got closer just to be on the safe side. So back to the room he went to get some rest and do some more reading. Day after day and night after night, Big Dred continued with his plan and before you knew it, those months became weeks, then weeks became days. He was determined and focused. He had not even realized that he was down to two months before his release from prison. He knew it was down to the wire and he had difficulty containing himself.

"Man, damn homie. What you so happy 'bout?" his roommate asked, sounding annoyed and jealous.

"It's 'bout that time, homie. I'm down to two months before I'm out of this joint," Big Dred boasted.

"Well, if you have two months or less before your release, then you need to go get your pre-release packet."

"Pre-release packet?"

"Yeah, homie, it's time to pull out the list of things to do before your scheduled released date."

"Like what?"

"Classes, physical, placement in work release and clothes for release. Man, don't be acting like you don't know… you know the routine, this ain't your first rodeo."

"I guess you're right, bro'; but man, hell, I forgot. But anyways, that's what's up. I'll get on that in the morning."

"Just go set up your pre-release meeting with your counselor and she'll take care of the rest."

After that bit of advice, Big Dred called it a night so he could get up early to meet with Mrs. Cameron.

Chapter 10

Big Dred slept well. He jumped from his tiny cell bed feeling chirpy but immediately remembered the list of things he had to get out of the way prior to his release. His routine, however, was the same; but he went through the chores with the lingering list on his mind… complete a pre-release class along with his meeting with Mrs. Cameron to conduct his verification of residence, halfway house assignment, his transportation from the institution, and check to confirm his clothing list before it was sent to the R/D unit. So he straightened up and headed for her office to get them out the way.

Upon entering the office, an antique three by four foot bulletin board with a sign-in sheet attached grabbed his attention. Big Dred quickly glanced over the sheet and found a time that was suitable and wrote his name in that particular slot. As soon as he was finished and began to walk away, he saw Mrs. Cameron approaching him.

"Yes, Mr. Patson, you looking for me? How can I help you?"

"Yes, ma'am, I'm trying to set up my meeting for my pre-release. I signed up to come see you at eleven thirty tomorrow morning."

"It's almost that time."

"But it's for tomorrow."

"Well if you want to wait until tomorrow, fine; but I can take care of you now."

"Now?"

"Are you ready? Well, I guess you're not ready then, huh?" she calmly said.

"No, I don't have my paperwork."

"Ok, then. See ya tomorrow."

"Yeah, I can't wait either."

"I bet; I'll see you tomorrow at eleven thirty." Big Dred headed back to his room, almost skipping. Then the deafening sound of the siren disturbed the air, followed by a frightening voice over the intercom repeatedly yelling,

"Lockdown!"

He paused, trying to figure out what was going on. Inmates were scattering in every direction trying to get to the 'safety' of their cells before the doors were closed.

"Lockdown?" he thought to himself. What the hell was that about? Still trying to gather his thoughts and walking fast, he was trying to figure out what could have happened on the compound. But as he approached the corner adjacent to his cell, he noticed a number of officers standing at the entrance. As you can imagine, he froze. Panic set in temporarily but he was soon relieved of his fear when the officers did not turn their attention to him or initiate any interrogation. But he was still trying to understand what was going on and what to do. He was sure, though, that something really bad was going on. He continued to approach his cell, then he heard someone shout,

"Patson!"

He spun around to see who it was.

"Yeah!" he responded nervously.

"Are you Patson #55569-123?" the officer asked firmly.

"Yes I am, who wants to know?"

"Special Investigations Specialist Lieutenant Smith. I need to speak with you."

"What happened… why you need to speak to me?" "It's in reference to your roommate."

"My roommate?"

"Yes, where were you about thirty minutes ago?"

"Man, shit, I just came from my counselor's office."

"You sure?"

"Hell, yeah, I'm sure! Man, I don't need no trouble. You see, I'm trying to go home in a few weeks."

"Well, that's all fine and good but right now you need to follow me. Besides, you can't stay in your room and I need to verify this alibi."

"Shit, do you. I'll wait."

"I know, I plan to, but for now, follow Officer Bob to 'the shoe' (solitary confinement) since everyone is on lockdown and your room is the crime scene. There will be no movement until this investigation is complete."

"But I have a meeting in the morning with Mrs. Cameron."

"Well, looks like you will just have to reschedule it, son. Please let us do our job. And like I said, your bunk is part of an investigation and you can't stay in there."

Big Dred was confused but more pissed. Not only did he get thrown into solitary confinement, but he had absolutely no idea what the hell was going on or why that was happening to him. He was going to miss his meeting and that would severely compromise his release process. All he had on his mind was getting out. And the time he was getting ready to spend in confinement was something he wasn't trying to get accustomed to. He pleaded over and over not to be sent there but he had no choice. He knew that he would be forced to sit there until the lockdown was over. It was torture behind those four cement walls. Being forced into that small space for not one or two days but two long weeks was crazy. But just knowing that he missed his meeting along with all the other things he was set to do to prepare for his release drove him mad. For a moment, everything seemed to be falling apart again. Tiana even began to worry because he hadn't called her or his mother for days. She even drove out to the location for her weekly visit only to be turned away.

It took the institution two weeks to lift the lockdown and release the inmates back on the compound, but it took them an extra three days for Big Dred to be released because his room had to be sanitized and purged from the incident that had occurred in there. There was blood spattering and other pieces of evidence all over the room that required thorough cleansing. He pondered every minute on his impending release and the more he thought about it, the more excited he became. He rolled from his pint-sized bed, did his chores and made a few bold steps; he wasn't quite sure how or what to feel, nor what to say. But he kept walking… big man wasn't about to let this day go by in vain. As soon as Big Dred was finally released from confinement and began heading back to the dorm, he was approached by a few of his homies who began questioning him about the incident in his cell.

But Dred wasn't concerned… that was the last thing on his mind and he was only thinking about one thing: Getting Out! He was concentrating on his meeting with Mrs. Cameron so he could start the countdown. Hence, he continued to ignore all the questions and commotion going on around him and rushed back down to Mrs. Cameron's office to see if she was available.

As he entered the hallway leading to her office, he read the bulletin board notice: MANDATORY STAFF MEETING at three o' clock.

"Damn!" was all he could think of saying. He was horrified that things might go wrong on the actual day of his release. Nothing was going right. Disappointed, he turned and slumped away, thinking about how this was going to set him back and hinder him from being with Tiana. Heading back to his bunk, he decided to make one more stop at the medical center to see if he could schedule his lab and bloodwork since now he only had one month and two weeks left before it was time for his release. He figured there had to be something or someone that could help him. The walk seemed to take forever but he made it just in the nick of time. Big Dred entered the room and the nurse's assistant had him sign in and have a seat.

"Ma'am, excuse me, but is Nurse Savoy available? he asked.

"I'll check, she replied.

"May I ask who is looking for her?"

"Patson!"

"Ok, Patson, give me minute."

And as she reached to the back to locate Nurse Savoy, he stood there waiting patiently.

"Mr. Patson!" someone yelled from the back.

"Have you eaten yet?"

"No, why?"

As Nurse Savoy made her way to the front, she grabbed a packet for him.

"Mr. Patson, slide over here to the end of the counter." She then began to explain to him that he needed to be fasting for his blood work and labs.

"No ma'am, I haven't eaten all day."

"Well, are you ready to do this now, because it's going to take at least a week or two to get these results back and you're due to be released around that same time frame."

"I know and I'm ready."

"Well let's do it then; follow me."

So the nurse's assistant escorted Big Dred to the patient waiting area to prep him for the bloodwork. And, after thirty-five minutes, Big Dred finally had something he could check off on his 'to-do' list.

Now he could finally head to his room and pack. Really wasn't much to go through or pack up anyway due to the fact that the room had been ransacked and torn apart from the incident weeks prior. Plus, his only worldly possessions were a few tattered underwear, about three undershirts, a discolored almost bristle-less toothbrush, an old chipped hairbrush, a scarf and a few other small items... just enough for the little brown box under his arm. There wasn't anything to do but give away his prison gear and live out of his bag for the next couple of weeks until he was scheduled to go home… home sweet home.

As you can tell, the home stretch was near. He stayed on top of everything that needed to be done. He finally met up with Mrs. Cameron for his final class and checklist. All that was needed now was his clothes to wear home. Things were back on track with a week left to spare.

Both he and Tiana were excited and the arrangements had been set. The best part of all this was that he was going straight home. No halfway house, no probation, no restrictions…. nothing. Again, his excitement started to balloon and he wanted to call home to see how things were coming along and to find out what time Tiana was coming to pick him up. But there was only one problem: his mobile phone account had already been shut off. It was official, down to the wire. He hurried to Mrs. Cameron's office to see if she had gotten his paperwork in from Nurse Savoy and if she would let him make a phone call. He was dying to find out what needed to be done if his results weren't back in time and also to call Tiana to confirm his pick-up time. The conversation was quite simple; she said she would allow him to make that call and reassured him that he would be notified in time… or so she thought. But as he picked up the phone and began to dial the number, Mrs. Cameron quickly stopped him.

"Patson, sit for a minute; let's talk. Are you ready? Do you have everything in order for your departure?" she queried.

"Just about," Big Dred replied.

"I'm calling to confirm my ride now for Tuesday. The only things needed to be taken care of are my test results from my physical and bloodwork. By the way, have you heard anything yet?" he remembered and asked.

"No, but I didn't realize that you were leaving on Tuesday, either."

The conversation went back and forth for a few more minutes with Big Dred emphasizing that he was ready to go, getting a bit aggressive at times. Mrs. Cameron wanted him to know how much she cared about him, and that he should be careful out there. But when she told him that, he became a bit concerned and kept asking her why she said that. She explained that it was nothing serious, but he should be wary of his surroundings, be mindful of who he associated with, that honesty and respect work both ways, and that he should be careful of how he treats others around him, especially when feelings are involved. He promised her he would. While digesting these wise words, he suddenly realized that someone had picked up the phone because the shouting was quite audible from the other end...

"Hello, hey, what's good?" he asked the caller on the line.

"Hey Derric!" the caller said,

"Who's this?" he replied.

"This is Sophie."

"Sophie... oh, what's up girl? Where's Tiana?"

"She's in the shower, can you call her back?"

"Nah man, just tell her I need to see her bright and early Monday morning. My phone account has been turned off and closed out since I'm leaving on Tuesday."

"Ok, I will let her know."

"Ok, thanks!" And just like that, the conversation was over and he got off the phone. But before walking away, Big Dred had a few words to exchange with Mrs. Cameron.

He wanted to thank her and let her know how much he appreciated her for all her help. She made him feel like somebody… not just a number… and that he still mattered regardless of his situation. She reminded him to take care of himself and not to spend that money on B.S., advising him to invest, to get a business, to live and enjoy life.

He gave her a handshake and a 'see ya later' glance, then he walked from her office. He was relieved. He finally felt like things were moving in the right direction. Three more days and he was home free. So as the weekend approached and Big Dred took his time saying his goodbyes, he laughed and joked with his buddies, gave away the rest of his 'belongings' and waited patiently for Tuesday's arrival. He went to bed early both days to make the time go faster… well, so he thought.

Then the alarm pierced the early morning silence. It was Monday morning; the sun was barely peeping out but sun or not, he was ready and no power in Heaven nor earth was stopping him. He had served his time and paid his dues; he was ready to go! He was now exactly twenty-four hours away from his release and to be locked tight in Tiana's arms along with the kids and his mom.

"Patson! Visit!" someone shouted over the intercom.

As if he didn't already know, he rushed from the unit so he could see the love of his life. It had been a couple of weeks since they last saw each other because of the lockdown. He had so much to say to her but it didn't really matter since they would have the rest of their lives to talk. With a pep in his step, glitter in his eyes and a childlike smirk on his face, Big Dred skipped into the visitation room and checked in at the front desk where there was a message waiting for him. The message stated that he needed to report to his counselor's office immediately after the end of visitation. Not the least bit worried, he proceeded toward the area where he expected

Tiana to be sitting. She was right there! Like a playful toddler he sprang into her arms where they locked into a tight embrace. With a warm smack on her lips they sat huddled in a corner where they chatted excitedly. They spent all day together, laughing, talking and planning for his arrival tomorrow. Man, were they excited. They were so excited that they didn't even realize that there was an announcement signaling the end of visitation.

"Man, that seemed like a quick visit," Tiana said as they both jumped up attempting to head towards the desk.

He walked fast, pulling Tiana to the desk and he waited for them to escort her out. He didn't want to give them any reason to detain him whatsoever. He then turned around and directed his attention toward Mrs. Cameron's office. He scurried along because he knew this had to be important. Maybe it was finally the news he had been waiting on. By the time he got to the entrance of her office, he was almost breathless. Big Dred stood there a bit agitated, still wondering… He knocked gently, then a little louder since there was no response. He paused then resumed knocking, only to find out that Mrs. Cameron had already left for the day.

"Damn!" he shouted in frustration, wondering what the hell he should do since he was scheduled for release in the morning. Angry and frustrated, he walked back to his unit for the last night. He already said his final farewells and gave away the remainder of his personal items except for what he needed in the morning. So he showered, put his few pieces of personal items together when he was done and lay on his bunk until he was out for the count. The alarm sounded the next morning and he jumped up, stretched his arms upwards, closed his eyes as if he was praying, then a crooked smile lit up his face. The day had arrived. He did a quick two-minute workout, slipped on his slides, grabbed his bag and raced to R/D to put on his 'real/normal' clothes and await his ride. But as he began his walk, he decided to make a slight detour towards Mrs. Cameron's office just one more time to say goodbye and get his results. The only problem was that Mrs. Cameron wasn't scheduled to come in until nine o' clock and his release was at eight.

Totally disappointed, he headed on down to the R/D building to wait. Time was moving slowly and he was getting a bit skittish and impatient. He couldn't wait to hear his name blasting all over the intercom for the last time and for everyone to hear. He wanted to see Tiana sitting out there, waiting, smiling… But he knew he had to remain calm and patient. Prison teaches you that, you know. Suddenly, it happened… just as he had predicted, it happened. The whole scenario was playing out right in his head… The intercom had come alive, he heard his name, his baby was waiting for him…The day had come. It was time for his final farewell. Aagh… A closed chapter.

At 8:15a.m. on that cool Tuesday morning, a few droplets of rain, showers of blessings perhaps, danced across the huge yard and then stopped. The sun peeped out from the Far East as he stepped out, gingerly; glancing sideways, he hastily sniffed the cool morning air. He made about ten more steps, each bigger than the first. Big Dred was free!

Chapter 11

As Tiana stood at the back of the car, waiting patiently for the man she had fallen in love with to walk out of those huge, wrought-iron prison doors, she had her phone ready to record. Every time they swung open, she instantly became a little bobble-head doll, bouncing all over the place trying to catch a good glimpse of him emerging. Tiana waited and waited until finally the doors were ajar, then they were wide open, and out walked Big Dred with a brown cardboard looking box in hand. The way he rushed out, you would think someone was in hot pursuit. Barely having a chance to make it to the car, Tiana ran and dived into his arms. All the hugs and kisses were overwhelming and that was not even the tip of the iceberg. He wanted for them to reach their destination as quickly as possible so they could finally enjoy each other's company. Laughing, talking, touching, and teasing made their ride home an excitable, yet difficult, one. He wanted Tiana's ass so bad that he kept trying to get her to pull over but she wouldn't. She tried standing her ground and held out. Not that she wasn't yearning for him too, but she had a little more endurance… a woman thing, perhaps. All she had on her mind was getting that man home behind closed doors to explore his entire body. The more he played and fondled her, the heavier her foot became on the gas pedal. He was gently rubbing her thighs, pulling her panties to the side and caressing her moist clit. And without saying it, she was feeling damn good. Eyes rolling, lips quivering and making a hissing sound. As her temperature rose, so did every hair on her body. Her tiny pear-shaped nipples stood firm and popping through her blouse. And of course, that foot on the gas was becoming heavier and heavier by the minute, which would ensure a quicker time home.

Sixty miles an hour dashed to 90 miles in record time as the euphoric feeling reached its zenith. Then the wails of the sirens brought them back to reality. She glanced in the rear view and there they were… "Oh, shit

Derric! Stop it, damn. Now the police is pulling me over."

"So what? Just be calm. What you worried about? We're not doin' nothing wrong, we straight."

Tiana was nervous, but Big Dred didn't know why. He asked her again,

"We're straight aren't we?" "Damn!" she replied as the tears began to flow. And as Tiana decelerated and was pulling over, crying like a baby, she noticed the officer was right behind her. She was nervous as hell as the portly officer alighted from his cruiser and made his way to her side of the car. Big Dred began to talk pure shit. He was talking so much that Tiana began to panic even more. He was confused; he couldn't understand why she was so nervous when she had absolutely no reason to be. This was not the time to get scared, especially since they had just left the prison.

"Babe," she said, "Please don't be mad, but I forgot to put my gun up before I left the house and it's under my seat."

"What the Fuck! Ah man, damn. You trying to get a nigga fucked up and I'm not even home yet. Is it registered?" he asked.

"No!" she replied.

"This some bullshit, Tiana. What the hell were you thinking?"

Well, as she rolled down her window, the officer asked for her license and registration. She demanded of the officer his reason for the pullover. Of course, you know the officer wasn't even concerned at that point but he told her anyway.

"Speeding ma'am," he said. Then he asked.

"Where are you in a rush to?"

Tiana didn't respond at first. Then as the conversation went on for a few more minutes before Tiana decided to tell him where she was coming from, she told the officer she had just picked her man up from prison. Which allowed him to have a little bit of sympathy. He nodded and grinned and said,

"Don't hurt him," and let them go with a harsh warning. And just like that, Tiana and Big Dred were back at it again, riding down I-4 dying to reach home. But riding down I-4 was anything but peaceful. This man talked so much shit and asked so many questions that you couldn't help but to think this relationship was over before it even got started. You see, Big Dred was pissed, but he also realized she played it off smooth and got them off with just a warning. They were lucky as hell too, because if the police would have found that gun, both Tiana and Big Dred would have definitely been done. Then the ride became quiet with Big Dred staring out the window; he was looking so lost and out of place that you couldn't help but laugh at him. He began to notice all the changes that had taken place while he was locked away; he was obviously in shock. Just sliding down Highway 50 brought back so many memories for him that he couldn't help but wonder what the old neighborhood was going to look like.

First stop was at his mother's house where all his kids would be waiting for the big surprise. No one knew he was coming home except Tiana, Mimi (one of her roommates) and his mom. How Tiana managed to keep his homecoming such a big secret from her other two roommates was beyond me. As Tiana and Big Dred pulled into his mom's driveway, they noticed her car wasn't there, so they sat in the vehicle talking. Tiana and Big Dred had began to talk about the situation that just had taken place. He wanted her to know how bad she messed up and how things could have been worse and he could have easily landed him back in jail. She started to cry and became very apologetic. After a while he couldn't help but to forgive her since she had been the only chick in his corner for the last few years.

He pulled her close and kissed her gently and wiped her tears. He told her to get the gun and go put it up and that the first gift she was getting for her twenty-first birthday next year was a concealed gun class to get that gun registered. Then they began reminiscing about old times. He tried to get Tiana to remember some of the things that only they knew had happened when they had spent time together some years ago. By then, he was getting impatient so he had Tiana call his mom's phone to see where she was and how long it would take her to get back there. Mrs. Clark picked up the phone and assured that she was home and that her car was in the garage; a sense of peace overcame him and he thought to himself, this was truly the only place that looked and felt the same: his mom's house… this house would never change.

She came peeking out the window and rushed to open the door to greet and hug him, welcoming him home. They were all just so excited and swamped in his presence that she couldn't let him go. She hurriedly took him by the hand so that no one would notice him. Walking around in his mom's house, all he could do was savor the smell, the familiar aroma of some real, good old fashioned soul food. His major stop was in the kitchen just to confirm what his mom was cooking. He knew too well… damn that food smelled good! Finally, Big Dred was about to grub on what he grew up on all his life… his mom's authentic cuisine! But his mom wanted him to wait until the kids came over so they could eat as a family; he agreed but still he couldn't resist. He ran in the kitchen and took to those pots like a duck to water.

This ex-jail bird gulped ravenously; you'd thought he had never seen food all his life. After he was finished eating, his gut looked like he was eight months pregnant. Good food, good conversation, good people, good place... and just sitting around until the kids came home was all he had to do. But Tiana had other plans; she was still horny as hell from all the pussy-playing and caressing in the car on their way home.

"Wait! Wait! Wait a minute! How do you know all this stuff, Jay?" the doctor asked, looking a bit dreary.

"Just keep listening, it will all be revealed soon enough. So, can I finish?"

"Yes, sorry, continue." Anyways, as I was saying, Tiana was hot and horny. She wanted his ass real bad since he started all that playing and getting her aroused in the car; she wanted to feel him deep inside of her. They had been doing all that talking while he was in prison and now the time had come to pay the piper and see if he was really about that life, or he was all talk. There was just one problem with that.... it was not going down in Mrs.

Clark's house so he tried to brush Tiana off for the moment.

Naturally Tiana was quite pissed off, stormed out and went back to the car. As she sat in the back seat pouting like a three-year-old, playing on her cell phone and scrolling down her timeline on Facebook, she realized that someone had posted, "Welcome home Big Dred!" She froze. She was furious. She leaped from the car and ran to Big Dred showing him the post and asking him who else knew he was getting out today. Of course, you know he couldn't answer. But he was also curious to know if the kids and Meka knew.

"What is this?" he asked.

"Just read it."

No, wait, let me call the house and see if one of the girls knew about this."

Sliding the phone off Facebook and onto the keypad, Tiana was very upset. I don't see what the big deal was, the dude was home, and that was all that should have mattered to them. Sometimes females can be so emotional. You see, when Tiana got Brena, her other roommate on the line, she quickly flipped into beast mode. She drilled that poor girl, asking her if she had told anyone else that Big Dred was coming home. But with a quick response, Brena flipped it right back on her.

"First of all, what is the big damn secret? I'm trying to figure out why you didn't tell us in the first place. Yeah, I knew he was coming home, and you know who told me. You know Mimi talking ass can't hold water."

"Mimi told you?"

"Yeah, you know she was dying to. I also talked to Rick. You know he was sad that his buddy was out. But, as for the post on social media, that's not even my style."

"Well, we just didn't want anyone to know until the kids got home and got a chance to see him first. That's why we've been posted up at his mom's house all day."

"Whatever, Tiana, just do you. I think it was petty but it's cool."

The conversation confused Tiana, she didn't see why her roommate was mad at her for not mentioning that her man was coming home. Personally, that would have been the first red flag, but poor naïve Tiana brushed it off. They talked for a few more minutes before getting off the line. Just then, there was a knock on Mrs. Clark's door. The kids had arrived. Tiana and Mrs. Clark ushered Big Dred into the back room to wait until they came and got him. They wanted to get a picture of the kids' reactions and the almost historic reunion. Only when Mrs. Clark yelled, "Come on in!" and the door swung open, it wasn't the kids. Can you guess who it was?"

"Who was it?" the doctor asked. 'Hmmm… Baby-momma!'

Baby-momma Meka decided she would stop by and see her baby-daddy and hoped he was there alone. This man hadn't even been home a good eight hours before the tramps and skanks started flocking to his mom's front door like flies to dead meat. But what Meka wasn't expecting was Tiana to be sitting there in plain view. She looked eagerly around to see if he was there and then she asked Tiana where his mom was. Although

Tiana clearly knew who it was at the door, she still wanted Mrs. Clark to know.

"Momma, someone's at the door for you!" Tiana yelled. Entering the foyer.

Mrs. Clark inquired, "Who is it?"

She saw Meka but no kids. Understandably, she was angry.

"Uh, where are the kids, Meka?"

"They still at school. I came by first to make sure you still wanted them."

"Wanted them?" she admonished, getting very upset both at this rude comment and Meka's unwelcomed presence. And she let Meka have it. See, Meka was known for trouble and coming in with her 'thot' gear on.

Mrs. Clark knew just what time it was. She knew this hood-rat all too well and that she was there to try and seduce her son. She had an agenda and as far as Mrs. Clark was concerned, it wasn't happening.

"What you all dolled up for? Where you headed?" She asked.

"Well," Meka answered, shamefacedly, "I actually came over here to see Derric and talk to him briefly."

"Oh, no, ma'am, I'm sure you know I know better. What you got to talk to Derric about? Derric has been gone for three years and not once have you tried to talk to him. Please don't come over here starting that mess, Meka. Now go get my grandbabies and hurry up!"

"Mrs. Clark, I just wanted to give him a few dollars."

"A few dollars, where is it? You can give it to me and I'll make sure he gets it. Is that all?"

"I also wanted to let him know he has a place to stay."

"Oh, really now?' she laughed mockingly. "He has a place to stay for your information, Lil' Miss Meka. Take my advice, just keep it moving! Bye!"

Mrs. Clark didn't mince words and spared no time in letting Meka know that she was aware of her games.

"Meka, please go get my grandbabies and don't come back without them. You got my pressure all up with your foolishness."

Meka was mad, and even though she didn't like what Mrs. Clark had to say, of course she heard her loud and clear. After dismissing Meka, she wanted to talk to Big Dred and Tiana before the kids came back. She had him and Tiana come into the living room and decided she'd give them some words of wisdom, explaining to them how they needed each other and how they needed to be each other's best friend and support system. She wanted to make sure Tiana knew how to handle Meka and not let others interfere. Furthermore, she wanted Tiana to know what she was up against and that she was dealing with the baby-momma from hell. By then, Tiana was ready to go but they still had to wait for him to see the kids. She couldn't wait for this visit to hurry up and take place so they could go home…you already know what was on her mind. And since Mrs. Clark had told her how to deal with Meka, she couldn't help but wonder how she would act when she came back with the kids.

It was just crazy how Tiana didn't say much. However, she spoke and helped to surprise the kids. And well, just imagine Big Dred hiding until he was instructed to come out for the big surprise. And boy, when he finally emerged from that back room and his kids saw his face, they didn't know what to do. They were consumed with joy; it was very emotional to finally have their dad home with them. His daughter was equally surprised to see her dad in regular clothes and not in those prison blues that had her crying like a baby. It was a beautiful experience. After spending time with his kids, his mom and Tiana, they realized Meka had come back to pick up the kids. But Big Dred answered the door and was ready for war. He knew Meka was going to try and start some drama with him because of what his mom had said to her earlier. She was feeling some type of way but she still spoke.

He wasn't in the mood, though; he quickly cut the conversation short, after not speaking with each other for three long years. Besides, they were not romantically connected so what was there really to talk about? There was nothing to talk about. But after all the insults and shunning from both he and his mom, it didn't stop her from giving him three stacks.

"Wait, wait… what? What are three stacks?" the doctor questioned curiously.

"Money: three thousand dollars."

"What? Where did she get three thousand dollars to give him?"

"Doc, I don't know. I just know what I was told. And although she gave him the three stacks, it didn't change a thing."

"Oh, so he didn't take it?"

"Oh, he did take it! But not at first. But when he was reminded of where it came from and what was taken from him, he did and gave it to his mom. He told his mom it was the least Meka could have done, considering all that he had done and sacrificed in the past for her and the kids. He walked away from her and began walking the kids towards the car to say their goodbyes. Meka couldn't say a word; she just waited for them to finish getting strapped in and left. Now that they were gone, it was time for him and Tiana to get a move on since they had been over his mom's house all day. Time was winding down and it was getting late. Tiana was finally going to have that alone time she was dying for… to lay next to the man she had been longing for. Years of anticipation was finally becoming a reality. Tiana had loved this man from the age of fifteen and now he was hers, all hers, to have and to do whatever she pleased with. As they said their goodbyes to his mom and headed for the car, Tiana decided to call her mom to check on Chase before heading to the crib. She didn't want any interruptions or distractions of any kind. She had planned to take Big Dred home and give him a beautiful night to remember.

As they began the drive home, the music was setting the tone and the mood was right. I don't know what all went down on the ride home but it was obvious that sex was in the air, especially when the king of R & B was in heavy rotation. They weren't getting there fast enough, but they were definitely rushing trying to get there. They pulled into the parking lot of the complex that Tiana and her friends shared. She spared no time in making him know that she was ready to do what comes naturally, but she wanted Big Dred to know just how serious she was about him and how free she wanted to be and to have no worries, so she pulled an envelope from her purse with his name on it. The envelope had been sealed and waiting for him to open. "What is this?" he asked. Tiana had to refresh his memory of the plan to exchange paperwork (test results) when she got home so they would both be on the same page. There would be no secrets, no surprises. She wanted him to feel like he was able to have her in any possible way he wanted and vice versa. When he opened the envelope and read the results from the blood work and test, he realized his baby was clean: no diseases, no high blood pressure, no diabetes, no nothing. She was in picture-perfect health. He was so happy, he thanked her for being woman enough to care about their health by getting checked out and sharing it with him. But that joy and excitement quickly changed to disappointment.

"So, let's see yours, now," Tiana politely demanded.

"Where's yours?" she asked.

"I don't have it, baby, but let me explain…. My results didn't come back in time. I was released before my counselor came in. Does this change anything?"

"Well, yes and no. Yes, it changes the fact that we can't have sex without it. But no, it doesn't change how I feel or my love for you."

"So why can't we have sex, then? Do you think something is wrong with me? There is nothing wrong with me except I have high blood pressure." Big Dred tried to convince Tiana that she could trust him. He wanted her to feel like she had nothing to worry about. He also wanted to show her how serious he was about her. He pulled her closely and lifted her head while gazing into her eyes.

"Tiana, baby, you can trust me," he assured. He then tried kissing her but she stopped him. She told him she wanted to take their conversation inside.

Chapter 12

They alighted from the car hand in hand and ascended the stairs. Tiana felt that something was wrong; the mood had suddenly changed, the silence was uncomfortable… the atmosphere just didn't feel right as they entered the apartment. She didn't feel quite the same as she did before giving him the letter; she felt kind of awkward. Nevertheless, the conversation started up again. Tiana wanted answers, but Big Dred had nothing else to say. It didn't matter that she had concerns, but she wondered why he thought she was going to be an easy lay. Her mind started to question his motives; she couldn't understand why he would even consider thinking that she would give in without that paperwork. This made her nervous and she felt like this was going to cause a rift between them because of all the sudden arguing, yelling and shouting at each other. Their conversation was just like a roller coaster, going up and down. They were off to a bad start and they were just getting started; she thought she was about to lose him. This sudden change of events was unexpected. What was supposed to be a night of passion and romance to welcome her man home had turned out to be a shouting match, ending with them sleeping in separate rooms.

Big Dred sat on the couch while Tiana stormed off and bolted for her room. The separation had already been enough torture but to hear Tiana in the room crying, really made him feel bad. He didn't mean to hurt her; he just had to make it right. So he got up and headed down the hallway, following the sound of Tiana's crying. He made it to her door and stood there for a moment before knocking.

"Tiana, baby! Please open the door so we can talk about it. Please baby, let's talk."

But he got no response. He begged her to hear him out. And after a few more minutes of pleading, the door opened slowly and he was granted access. They sat on the bed and started up the conversation once again. Tiana tearfully tried to make Big Dred understand just why she was dead set against unprotected sex or being involved in any kind of sexual activity without proof that he was ok.

They talked on and on until they came to a mutual agreement of using protection until they were able to go to the doctor and get a full exam to get the results. Relieved by her decision, this lightened the burden, diffused the tension somewhat, and made him realize that he had a good woman and that Tiana was at least willing to try. Now he had permission to pull Tiana closer and began kissing her softly. She stopped him to grab the remote and turned some music on that must have done the trick because the mood had returned… the passion was re-ignited. He started to work from her lips, to her neck, to her nipples and eased down to her stomach. This was causing the expected adrenaline rush and both of them instantly became aroused. He stopped, jumped from the bed and stood before Tiana, pulling her to the edge. He then eased himself between her legs and got on his knees. He skillfully removed her panties and laid her on her back. Carefully, he guided his eager tongue, slurping, sucking, diving, stroking… he was making up for all those years all that he had missed… all that he was longing for. This man went to work. His tongue slid down her stomach to her navel and down again to her quivering pussy; with each long stroke from the tip of that tongue, he made Tiana moan for more.

The deeper he went the louder her moaning became. She wanted him and he wanted her. They couldn't deny the yearning for each other. They were submerged in passion and inundated by deep affection; the moment was theirs.

The more he ate her pussy, putting that head on her, the more she attempted to run; perhaps it was too much for her... she didn't want to run, but she attempted. She begged him to stop, a slight disingenuous begging that men knew wasn't real but was instead interpreted as the woman wanting more. It only made him intensify his actions. He whispered, "You want me to stop?" But she knew she didn't want that to happen.

"Doc, you ok? Am I making you uncomfortable?"

"Uh, umm... No, I'm ok, continue," he said.

I was hoping that I wasn't making him feel uncomfortable, but he was regaining great interest in my detailed account and urged me to please continue the story. So Tiana laid back and tried to take it like a big girl; whining, moaning and pleading him to "keep it right there babe, right there." He instantly knew he had her, he had hit her G-spot; because not soon after that, she locked down on him like she had a bitch in a head- lock to let him know she was cumin.' But it wasn't over yet. It was time... time to get it in. She hurried up and tossed him a condom and watched him put it on then allowed him to enter her slowly.

"Wait, so she had sex with him?"

"Yes Doc, she did. And I guess it got good to them and he couldn't take it anymore because the condom broke."

"Uh oh!" 'Uh oh' was right. Because when the condom broke and Tiana realized that she didn't have any more, she ended up giving in. She ended up having unprotected sex with him, forgetting all that she had said in their conversation earlier. All that talking went out the window; that's what good fucking does, I guess, as well as his promise to go to the doctor. Those two became inseparable, fucking early and often. She felt as if she was on cloud nine. Tiana finally had her man home, just as she dreamed it would be. She woke up to him and went to bed with him, playing wifey to him and all.

She became submissive, the whole nine yards, cooking, cleaning, laundry, fucking and sucking… you know all the wifely duties most married women do. This was the life she yearned for and while she was enjoying her new found status, two of her roommates no longer agreed. The third one named Sade had other things on her mind that she really didn't care. Day in, day out, week after week, Big Dred was always there. There was no room for the girls to breathe, hang out or do the things they did before he intruded their place. The partying, walking around as they pleased or just having the girl talks were all cut out, making this situation no longer cool. Their living situation had taken a downward turn. They had become very angry, distanced, cold and jealous of Tiana's man being home while their men were still locked up. All of a sudden, everyone wanted out; they just didn't know how to go about telling her that this arrangement wasn't working out. They never had a moment alone to themselves because Big Dred and Tiana were always together. They needed to let her know that they felt somewhat intimidated, but when was the question.

After several weeks of going back and forth, they were very vocal about their concerns to Tiana. And in doing so, they discovered that they would have the perfect opportunity when Big Dred attended a teacher parent conference for one of his kids with Meka. Finally, Tiana was alone and everyone would have a chance to talk as well as voice their concerns with their once roomie friend. The only problem was that Tiana had a doctor's appointment pre-scheduled that she couldn't miss. So, she promised the girls that immediately following her appointment she would come straight home since they said it was mandatory that they met. Needless to say, this is where things got a bit crazy. Tiana did come straight home after the doctor's appointment, as promised to meet with the girls. The only problem was that she didn't look anything like she did when she left that morning. It looked like she had been crying.

"Oh goodness; what's wrong, Tee?" Mimi asked. Tiana tried to ignore the question and quickly changed the subject. She wanted to get on with the meeting as they all had planned. They sat down and began discussing their issues within the house. They couldn't take Big Dred being there anymore… well, at least two of them.

This pissed Tiana off to know that they had been sitting around talking among themselves about her man and their relationship; it was simply unacceptable to her. So of course, you know this is when the arguing began; they couldn't agree on anything. Tiana became a ticking time bomb waiting to explode. She desperately tried to stay calm but when they got ready to comment on my nephew Chase, that's when it happened."

"What happened, Jay?" the doctor asked. "The bomb exploded, Tiana lost it. She read each one of the girls, one by one, letting them know just what time it was. Tiana spared no compassion when it came to their feelings. And after all the silent tug-o-war and disrespecting each other, they all came to a mutual agreement."

"And what was that?"

"Well, let's just say that by the end of their meeting, everyone would be going their separate ways. Instead of harmony in the house, there was mayhem. All the girls were angry and bitter towards each other and not on speaking terms. They ended the meeting and dispersed to their rooms. Tiana was overwhelmed with all that had taken place throughout the course of the day. She needed to vent to someone because she couldn't believe what had just taken place. But who? She tried calling Big Dred, but there was no answer. This frustrated her, but she tried not to let it show. At that point, she really didn't care about moving out because the news she had gotten from her doctor earlier simply meant that there were bigger and more important things to think about. She made several attempts to reach Big Dred, but still, no answer... no text or anything.

She thought to herself that something was wrong, but she tried not to panic. Watching the minutes ticking by agonizingly, she realized he should have been home by now since the conference was at noon and it was now well after six o' clock; so where could he be? Tiana began pacing the floor trying to figure out what the hell was going on. She couldn't take it anymore, so she called his mother to see if she had heard from or seen her son. But in the midst of their conversation, Tiana broke down. She was worried and couldn't figure out what was going on. Mrs. Clark tried to calm her down and explain to her that he was ok and that they needed to sit down, have a heart to heart talk and get an understanding as soon as he came home.

This made it a little easier for her to pull herself together. She thanked Mrs. Clark and ended the call. She thought about all the things that Mrs. Clark had told her and for some reason, it gave her the urge to call her mother. So she did. Her mom needed to know what was going on in her life. As Tiana made the call, she heard her mom say,

"Hello?" and she broke down again.

"Momma!" she said.

"What's wrong, Tiana, stop crying. What's the matter?"

It took all she had not to tell her mom but of course, you know that was impossible. She hesitated and fought the feeling; she took a deep breath and let the words flow,

"I'm Pregnant!" she said.

There was a moment of silence on the line before Michelle began to talk.

"Tiana, calm down," she said,

"What's the problem, why are you being so extra? Listen, first of all, congratulations! Now, I don't know who you think I am but let me ask you a question: You having sex, right?"

"Huh?"

"Tiana, you fucking, right? No protection right?"

"Ma, please."

"Just answer the question. Never mind... but if you thought for a second that this wasn't a possibility, then you need to hurry up and come back home cause you not as grown as you thought."

Tiana was pissed; however, she heard her mom loud and clear. They had a brief conversation and her mom reassured her that she'd be just fine and make sure the child's father was aware of the situation. Tiana knew this was going to be hard; he hadn't even been home six months. She knew this was going to be the topic of discussion just as soon as certain people got wind of it. Michelle and Tiana ended their conversation as Big Dred was walking through the door. She was saying goodnight when she noticed a difference in his appearance; this prompted her to hang up the phone and focus her attention on him. He had this guilty appearance which made Tiana nervous. Before she could ask him what was going on, he snapped like a hoe, yelling and screaming for no reason.

This confused her and with her fragile emotional state, coupled with the early stage of pregnancy, his behavior only exacerbated the situation. He tried avoiding Tiana at all cost, trying to dodge her and staying out of her reach. He grabbed some clothes and rushed into the bathroom before she could get a word in. In disbelief, Tiana sat at the foot of the bed, waiting patiently for him to return. She was trying to figure out what the hell had just happened. Realizing he was taking too long, she headed to the bathroom and shook the handle but it was locked. Then she knocked on the door but he wouldn't let her in. See, Tiana still didn't know what the hell was going on, but she would find out in due time.

So, when Big Dred finally decided to release himself from the bathroom, looking and smelling all fresh and clean, he seemed like a different person. I guess he washed all the attitude and bullshit right off. Now he was ready to talk; his whole demeanor had changed as if nothing was wrong. Tiana didn't know what to do. He was worried and apologetic that she was confused. Still she was determined to tell him about her day. From the heated discussion with the roomies who were now not speaking to one another, to the news of their new addition. She was not excited at all; Tiana was nervous of what he might say. She took a deep breath and then she began to speak. The conversation started off as expected, cool and calm like the calm right before the storm. Big Dred didn't care about the girls being mad or that they had planned to move out. He had already been making plans for them to move out just as soon as his money came through.

He had yet to tell Tiana of his plans and definitely of the fact that he had won a lawsuit while in prison. So you know it didn't bother him one bit; he just had to convince Tiana to stop worrying and reassured her that he would take care of her. Tiana got ready to bring up the doctor's visit and the baby news but for this ultra-sensitive topic, she had to take a different approach. The only problem was that like earlier, she again became emotional and began to cry. Because for some strange reason, she seemed to think it would tick him off, World War 3 would take effect, and sparks would fly when she told him. But thankfully to her surprise, it didn't. It was different. He was actually overjoyed and happy at the fact that Tiana was pregnant with his baby. He would have the chance to watch one of his children grow up right under his nose, since he had no plans of splitting from Tiana. So all that crying and worrying Tiana was doing was for nothing, because she was finally going to have a real family. It seemed like all the stress of the day was behind her. She felt relieved and happy once they had discussed that. Then he brought up the roomies situation again.

That's when all hell let loose again. It went from zero to one hundred in a wink!"

"What happened?" the doctor asked. He let it slip that the girls weren't truly her friends as they had proclaimed, and he made it known that one of the three had been trying to give him some pussy on the sly. They were just ashamed that he didn't pick up on the offer, and they were ready to turn the tables on him, letting him look like the villain. He told her they were jealous and couldn't handle the fact that they didn't have what he and Tiana had. So now, that's when the grits hit the fan… it was on and popping. It was pretty clear that it was time for my niece to start looking for new roomies as soon as possible; she hoped those other roomies weren't so low down and dirty… shit, getting male roomies may not be better either.

"Did Tiana confront the girls?" the doctor asked.

Oh, you know she did, but everybody was pointing the finger and playing the blame game. Big Dred tried to keep Tiana calm for the sake of the baby. All the turning up trying to fight was definitely not an option. So her cussing and yelling became her only form of venting at this point. She went from room to room turning over furniture and throwing things. It took her a moment to calm down, especially after he grabbed her and quietly escorted her into the bedroom. He began to explain to her that it had been going on for a while now. But she was curious to know why he was just telling her after so long; if it was going on like he said it was, that should have been brought up when it first happened. And knowing how she felt and what was going on in the apartment, she didn't know who to believe, what to believe and who to trust.

She asked him several times which one of those loose bitches had propositioned him, but he would not disclose. She had an idea of who it was but she decided to let it go. That's when she realized from that moment, it would strictly be all about family and creating a comfortable living environment for her baby, herself and by extension, her son and Big Dred.

Chapter 13

Things were beginning to look up for Tiana and Big Dred. They had become a power couple and everyone wanted to be like those two, especially those roomies. Jealousy was at an all-time high; the roomies were mad because they're relationship had gotten stronger. You see, they took a lot of trips... traveling, waking up in different hotels, hanging out, going to dinner every night, going to shows, hosting party after party and just enjoying him being on top again. And even though the roomies had gotten out of line at one point, they (Tiana & Big Dred) forgave them and included them in some things. He even treated the roomies to a few spa dates with Tiana. And although Tiana was confused about all that was taking place and where the money was coming from, she never questioned her man. She loved to spend money especially his money; he was taking care of her and Chase.

She was feeling like this was the life and, just enjoyed being his one and only, and being spoiled and pampered on a daily basis. But that wasn't even the half of it. After several weeks of waiting to hear from the attorneys, things finally came through. He received his settlement money and it was on from there. Life was moving forward and in a positive direction, and living with the roomies was no longer a burden. The girls were informed that Tiana and Big Dred were moving out, and he made sure that she gave them her portion of three-months rent in advance so it wouldn't cause them to break the lease.

He was resolute on creating a happy and stress-free environment for Tiana, and he wanted no one to cause any unnecessary drama around her; he wanted her to focus strictly on them and their new addition. And at four months pregnant, she was having a rough time. The usual morning sickness, fatigue, constant weight gain and constant hunger were at an all-time high. She, however, was basking in all the attention she was getting from her man. He made her feel special, like a queen, not letting her lift a finger. All she did was take it easy and take care of their new house and Chase. She even seemed more relaxed, Tiana was on cloud nine, a 'hitting-the-million-dollar-jackpot' kind of feeling. Clearly, she couldn't have it any better. She was a totally different person with him and it was obvious… Tiana, my dear niece, was in love again! And in spite of everything, I was sincerely happy for her. We were a huge family and we were always doing things together. Holidays were very important for us; Christmas was just like any other special holiday that we always spent together. This one wouldn't be any different, except that we finally would have the opportunity to meet Tiana's mystery man; and boy oh boy, we couldn't wait… well, I know I couldn't. We were finally going to meet the man that she was having a baby with, as well as the one I had been hearing about who always kept a smile on her face.

As the family gathering was under way, we all did what most regular families do. We laughed, we talked, we ate, played games and watched old home movies. And just as we were prepared to do the gift exchange, the door swung open and Chase dashed inside to see his grandma. A few moments later, Tiana came wobbling in, hand in hand with her Mystery Man, aka Derric, aka Big Dred. My mouth hit the floor.

"Your mouth hit the floor?" the doctor asked. Yes, remember, he was a mystery up until that point."

"Oh yeah, ok, got you."

So, yeah, my mouth hit the floor; I was in disbelief. I didn't even know how to respond to or accept the truth, knowing how to even respond to the fact that Tiana's mystery man had been the man she was in love with as a teenager. Not only that…. this was someone I had met with another friend of mine a few weeks ago when he gave us V.I.P. access at the club. He paid for drinks and took us out to dinner, I mean breakfast, afterwards, and they were all over each other at the restaurant. We even went back to his suite and had some fun until we fell asleep. I was in total shock. I couldn't believe my eyes. And as Tiana was introducing him to everyone around the room, I just stood there and stared.

Tiana and I had not spoken in almost a year and a half and I didn't think that this day would've been any different, but it was. As they made their way towards me,

I sat straight up in my chair, thinking to myself, "Damn, this dude is still fine." It had been a minute and whatever he did or was doing to maintain his physique, man that shit was working."

"Seemed you had a crush on him, hmmm?' the doctor joked.

"You don't even know the half, Doc. But anyway, as they got closer and Tiana stared at me and proudly introduced him; I brushed the crumbs from my hands and made a polite wave. As he and I made eye contact it seemed that he recognized me but tried to play it off; he spoke and acknowledged that it had been a long time, which I definitely agreed. We began to have a lighthearted, frivolous conversation, reminiscing about the past and that the last time I saw him was the day he caught his case a few years back and how devastated Tiana was. Now at this point I felt bad.

"You felt bad?" the doctor asked.

"Yes I did."

"Why?"

"Because I had just sat there and lied. Lied about how long it had been and the last time I had saw him. Not to mention if my calculations served me right, he had cheated on Tiana with my girlfriend just a few weeks prior. Man, I wanted so badly to be nosey but it just wasn't the time nor the place, so I played it off and initiated an animated discussion with her. We hugged and began to talk and apologized for the past.

It was the first time in a long time that I really realized that my niece was no longer a child but a grown woman. Her conversation was also more mature, and her thought process was seriously elevated. How I missed my niece, and although we would never get back to where we were, this conversation was proof that we had buried the past and moved on… I considered it growth. As we joined in with the rest of the family, I was compelled to hug her again. It felt good to have my niece and best friend back, and our annual Christmas family gathering truly felt complete... well, almost. We were having such a terrific time that we didn't even realize how late it was. Even Big Dred was enjoying himself; it had been years since he had been around family for the holidays so he was taking full advantage of making these moments memorable, and making them count. That is, until he got that phone call. It must have been very important because he stepped out for a moment to have more privacy. But when he came back inside, he suddenly had to leave.

He pulled Tiana to the side to speak to her in private and whatever he said she obviously really didn't take kindly to it. A big argument ensued and the next thing we knew, he was leaving. I just remember him whispering in her ear,

"Baby, stop tripping, I'll be back. I love you!"

He kissed her and hurried out the door. Tiana tried hard to continue having a good time but whatever he said to her had her mind uneasy. I didn't know what was going on but I know her whole demeanor had changed; and when I asked what was wrong, she didn't want to talk about it. That's when I decided to have my own heart to heart talk with her. I had to let her know that despite the past, I would always be there for her and would always be an ear to listen. Of course, she thanked me and assured me that meant a lot. I could see that Tiana was an emotional wreck. Her mind was unstable and she wanted to talk but she just kept on procrastinating, repeating that was not the time nor place. Just imagine my reaction when she said that; it threw me for a loop, but I let it go.

After another two and a half hours, Big Dred was back to pick up Tiana and Chase. But not before coming in and giving out a few gifts, saying his goodbyes and helping Tiana with her stuff. To constantly see my niece with a smile was rare, so I knew it was because of him. I wanted to capture that moment, because I wasn't sure if I would see her so happy and composed again. He was determined to keep her happy and maintain that smile on her face. Don't ask if I was excited for her. My thought was, "Had she found Mr. Right?" Only time would tell. He seemed to be a real gentleman even though I still had my suspicions about him; I just prayed I was wrong about him. Especially since I had this big question mark in the back of my mind now. I wanted to try hard to forget what I knew. It seemed to be all good, and things looked promising for them. Every day birthed something new, something different, new experiences, new ideas and new found happiness. My niece was content. Everything was going good in my opinion. Then, round about her seventh month check-up, I remember getting a call early one particular morning. Tiana said she wasn't feeling her best. Big Dred had gone to work and she needed a ride to the doctor. I didn't hesitate to take her. I dropped her off and returned for her within the next two hours. I actually got back a few minutes earlier just to make sure she didn't have to wait.

As Tiana emerged from the doctor's office, I noticed a kind of familiar distant, dazed countenance, one I had seen years before, but had not seen it since she got with Big Dred; and was terrifying to see it again. It was almost as if she had seen a ghost. It had me puzzled. So I figured that perhaps she had received some unfavorable news. I immediately alighted from the car and began walking towards her to help her maneuver her way back to the car, but she hesitated. I asked her if she was alright and she just stared at me, blank. A sad expression overcame her, an indication that all wasn't well in paradise. I asked her several times but with each question I asked, the answer remained the same… nothing. Tiana would not say a word. But I was not giving up. I told her that I would not move the car until she talked to me.

"Auntie, what do you want to know?" she asked.

"What's wrong with you?" I replied.

"Is it the baby? Are you ok? What's the matter? What did the doctor say?" She told me she didn't want to talk about it; she just wanted to go home. She kept saying that she needed to talk to Big Dred, but still I pleaded, over and over with her to tell me something. I wanted to help. She became cold and wanted me to stop asking questions and just take her home. She wanted to be in the privacy of her home where she could be alone to think things over, and have a conversation with Big Dred. That was not the place nor appropriate environment. She did divulge, however, that the baby was ok.

I reassured, "It's ok, Tiana, I know it can be overwhelming and nerve wrecking to know something maybe wrong with the baby, but you will be ok… the baby will be ok. You know your family got you. And I'm here no matter what."

Upon hearing that, she could no longer fight back the tears, she broke down. I grabbed her and hugged her tightly, then walked her to the side of the car. We sat there and talked for a little while. I reaffirmed our commitment to be there for her no matter what. Mid-way in our conversation, her phone rang. I knew it was Big Dred from the ringtone and from the sound of his voice, he seemed so excited to hear the news from the doctor as he began to talk to Tiana. Even though I knew she had just lied to him, clearly something wasn't right. Either she didn't want me to know or it was too much to talk about over the phone. He told her he had a big surprise for her and he couldn't wait for her to get home to see it. And although he said all of that, it didn't change the expression on her face. Deep down, something else was really bothering her, something she didn't want to talk about. I didn't want to harass her anymore, so I hurried and drove her home. We were entering the drive-way when we saw Big Dred and noticed that he had company.

It pissed Tiana off to see the cars in the yard when she was already upset. I knew then that this wasn't going to be pretty so I tried to calm her down before she got out of the car because I didn't want her stressing herself over the situation. I advised her to take some deep breaths to relax. The car door swung open and she made her way out and we noticed Derric coming outside with a smile on his face. I sat there for a moment in an attempt at giving them their privacy, thinking to myself,

"Man, this guy really loves my niece; he really cares about her." They had a nice home. I kept trying to figure out how they were able to afford all that. He had moved them into a baby mansion; it was huge. And this was just from the outside looking in; I could only imagine what the inside looked like. It was beautiful. But my thinking was cut short from all the screaming and shouting. I jumped out the car to see what all the commotion was about only to find out that Tiana's anger had ruined the surprise. This man had purchased not one but two brand new 6 series BMWs, black with the peanut butter brown interior to be exact, one for him and one for her. Her car still had the big red bow on it. I was standing there like a deer in headlights saying to myself,

"Damn, can you say upgrade?" But Tiana didn't care; she was more concerned about where the money had come from. I really didn't know what was going on but I couldn't believe she was being ungrateful. Soon, all the neighbors gathered outside, curious to find out what was going on. I was confused as hell; I couldn't believe what was going on. I was even more surprised at Tiana's reaction. It didn't sound good and so I urged them to take the conversation inside.

But, what I didn't realize was that part of the reason for the arguing was because this one particular car kept riding by, slowing up as if they were trying to get some attention. The tint was too dark to look inside but we all knew the horn worked from all the incessant hooting. I turned and began walking towards the back of my car to get a better look because the vehicle looked familiar. And just as I reached the back of the car, I realized who it was; and now that I knew, I wanted to know why they were making a scene. But they pulled off when they noticed me approaching their car. I stood there for a second to see if they were going to return and return they did. This time they rolled down the window and just as I had suspected, it was none other than Meka. Now, I wanted to know, why was Meka riding by this house? What did she want? I had no idea but I would soon find out because she started beckoning me towards the car.

"She knew who you were?"

"No, she didn't know my name, she just kept asking, 'Excuse me, excuse me, can you come here please?' So, I did. I didn't know what she wanted but at this point, I was even more determined to find out. And as I bent down to see what she wanted I heard Big Dred telling her to go head on and get from in front of his house.

Now I was really confused… for one, I didn't know why she would be looking for him and two; how the hell did she know where they lived and three, why the hell was he so hostile? Something wasn't right. Big Dred came rushing to the car trying to get her to leave but the more he tried to get her to leave the more attention she wanted. So she put the car in park and opened the door but when she stepped out and came around to the passenger side; as usual, all hell broke loose. Ms. Meka made it perfectly clear what she was doing there and now Tiana and I did, too. It was obvious and plain to see that Meka was pregnant, her baby bump wasn't quite as big as Tiana's but it definitely was there. But what really made this situation become worse was when Meka told us what was going on and why she was there. She wanted to see if we knew that she was pregnant with Big Dred's baby. And that she was tired of keeping it a secret. He was supposed to be taking Meka to have an abortion but she had refused when he jumped on her and given her a black eye.

The two of them took their arguing to another level and almost came to blows. It was hard to watch this play out in front of our eyes. Whatever it was, though, it seemed to be definitely the icing on the cake. Those words went deep, hitting Tiana like a ton of bricks; we both were in shock. I asked her to repeat it, and she did. It couldn't be but she said it again; and they say truth is stranger than fiction. But, whether this was fiction or not… we were hearing alright. She said she was pregnant with Big Dred's baby and she was keeping it. Tiana played it cool and stayed calm, but I knew better; I knew she was pissed. Not only was she pissed but she was crushed; her heart was broken. The arguing turned from Big Dred and Meka to escalating between Meka and Tiana. He was in the middle, standing between them looking stupid with not even a word to say. I was shocked and getting just as pissed off by the second. I knew he was too good to be true. I grabbed Tiana and hauled her away, advising her not to argue. I explained to her that even though this bitch wasn't shit, that in actuality Tiana's beef was not with her but with him. I tried convincing her to get some clothes and come with me but, she refused. She kept telling me she would be ok and that she would call me if she needed me. I had to get out of there and since my begging and pleading weren't having any effect, I hugged her and wiped her tears and left.

As I pulled off, my phone started ringing. The caller I.D registered Tiana's number, but when I picked it up, it was Big Dred trying to explain. At that point, I had absolutely nothing to say. All I kept thinking about was what I knew and kept from Tiana and what I had just witnessed. I tried cutting the conversation short but the more I asked him where my niece was, the more he tried to get me to listen, the more I ignored him. I wasn't having it. After the third time of him begging to let him explain, I eventually lost it! I cussed him out and demanded that he put Tiana on the phone. As soon as she picked up the phone, I asked her if she wanted me to come back, but her response was the same. I left it at that and hung up. I was beyond pissed and wanted so badly to go back and show this dude just how angry I was, but I couldn't. I didn't want Tiana to feel like I was trying to fight her battle even though she knew I told her I would always have her back. I had to respect what she said and try my hardest not to get involved.

Chapter 14

I headed home to a restless night with Tiana and this whole ordeal on my mind. So the next day, I called to check on things but I was in for a surprise… only it wasn't a good one. To my dismay, Tiana told me that after all she did for him and being loyal to him, after everything was exposed, she had no choice but to ask him to leave."

"Exposed, what you mean by exposed?" the doctor asked.

"Man, you wouldn't believe it. Tiana said they had a long talk and she found out a lot of things that she was unaware of and as a result, she no longer trusted him. This dude had been cheating on her from the start; he was a liar and a cheater who had stepped out on her several times since he had been home. She said what she didn't understand was how he was able to pull that off since they were always together. That's when she found out about the money he had won from his settlement while in prison: one point two million dollars this man had won when the ceiling collapsed on him. I couldn't believe what I was hearing. Tiana trusted him and he betrayed her. That made me very angry. I didn't know if it was because he had been with several different women or the fact that he was still a whore after all these years. Guess you could call him a wolf in sheep's clothing. Hence the maxim that, a leopard never changes its spots is so true! I asked her if she knew any of the women. She said no… Negative! But only time would tell. I was concerned and a little thrown off by that last remark, so I asked her what she meant by that statement but she chose to ignore me by changing the subject.

As the conversation continued, I could tell she had been crying; she seemed to be the least bit worried. We continued to talk for a few more minutes when the weirdest thing happened. I heard a loud thud, a crash and a boom, then the phone went dead. I jumped up, calling her name, I yelled, "Tiana, Tiana… Hello? Tiana!" but there was no answer. I hung up then attempted to call her back. I dialed her number several times but each time it went straight to her voicemail. Fumbling through the house trying to find my shoes, I got my thoughts together. I grabbed my purse and darted out the door, jumped into the car and headed straight to her house. All I kept thinking about was if this dude had hurt my niece and how I was going to become a permanent resident of the D.O.C."

"The D.O.C., what's that?"

"The Department of Corrections, Doc."

"Oh, o-ok, continue."

"I didn't have Big Dred's number to call him to see if he was really there, so I began to panic. I was scared as hell trying to figure out what was going on but I knew I had to get there. I was doing ninety all the way trying to make sure my niece was ok. I was so glad the police were nowhere in sight because I would have been going straight to jail that night. I was hauling ass, and just as I turned on my niece's street, I tried calling her again. Still, no answer. I remember the street was peaceful and didn't seem as if there had been any kind of disturbance. I whipped into the yard and jumped out the car. It was still running but I didn't care because I needed to get inside. As I approached the entrance, I heard Chase screaming at the top of his lungs as if someone was trying to hurt him. I knocked on the door, no answer. I rang the doorbell, no answer. I yelled Tiana's name, but still no answer. I was freaking out because I know someone had to be inside the house because that baby was screaming bloody murder.

Slowly, I began walking around the house peeking through the windows trying to find something open, but everything was tightly secured. As I got to the side of the house by the garage, I saw an empty pot sitting next to the door. It seemed quite odd to me at first but then I thought to myself that if Tiana was anything like her dad, she would have a hiding spot somewhere outside here.

"Think Jay," I said to myself. If it was my brother, where would be his hiding place… where would it be? Where? With this in mind I took a chance by going over to the pot and peeped inside, but nothing. I was so angry that I kicked it over, and lying underneath it was a piece of metal sticking halfway into the ground. Bingo! A key! But a key to what, to where? Well, I didn't care, I just grabbed it and began checking doors. But the key was not working, I didn't know where else to check. I checked all the doors but nothing. I became a frantic crazy woman standing outside as Chase cries got louder and louder. I didn't know what to do at this point; I was standing there contemplating my next move.

As I started pacing back in forth I looked down and the next thing I remember is grabbing one of the bricks sitting next to the flower pot and praying that it didn't hit Chase as I put that muthafucka through the big glass sliding door. Now, finally, access granted. I darted inside and started looking for Chase. I heard his screams but I didn't see him. Then I yelled his name and sure enough, there he was dashing towards me! Covered in blood from head to toe, I lost it. I didn't know what to do. I picked him up and tried calming him down but he was just pointing down the hallway. There was something he wanted me to see. So I eased him back down and holding his hand, I carefully and nervously followed his tiny frame down the hallway. My heart was pounding and there was fear in his innocent eyes. Then I saw what appeared to be two feet half protruding from the bathroom. I panicked… I was almost breathless as I held onto Chase's tiny hand as we shuffled our way toward the entrance. And there she was, lying in a pool of her own blood… my niece, Tiana. I grabbed a towel and tried to figure out where to put it but I couldn't identify the source of the bleeding. I tried checking her pulse but I couldn't find one. She wasn't breathing either and I lost it. My screams were piercing, they echoed along the hallway. Poor Chase knew something had gone terribly wrong upon seeing his mom lying there and then my subsequent reaction. But I guess he couldn't really fathom precisely what the situation was. I couldn't believe my eyes; I didn't know where all the blood was coming from. I hurried up and dialed 911 after which I called her mom and told her to meet us at the hospital. I was calling everyone I could think of that could possibly know or have a number for Big Dred, but there was no luck.

No one knew where he was or how to reach him. I stood over my niece with my nephew in my arms looking at her lifeless body. I heard a knock on the door; it was the paramedics coming to the rescue. I opened the door and moved out the way. After a brief conversation with one of them, trying to explain the situation, they suited up and placed her on the gurney and instructed me to follow them to the hospital. I got Chase a few more diapers and milk, jumped into the car and sped off. I stayed right behind the ambulance just as I was told. The news must have spread like wildfire because by the time we were pulling into the emergency room, a few friends and family members had already gathered, waiting, visibly shaken, sobbing and in disbelief. You would have thought that Tiana was some celebrity. It was an outpouring of raw emotion. I found the family some seats in the waiting area and I held my nephew tightly, sat there and just began to pray. I prayed for God to intervene and work a miracle, and for the doctors to find out what had happened to have left Tiana in such a horrible condition. I prayed for my darling nephew, and I begged God to heal Tiana and not let her die. I was truly overwhelmed with what was happening that I didn't realize my phone was ringing.

It was my best friend on the line. She was calling to check on me and to see if I were up to some drinks. But as soon she realized that this was no play, tragedy was in the air. I was hollering and my speech became incoherent. She kept asking what was wrong, but I just couldn't answer. She wanted to speak to someone else around me to find out what was going on so I handed my brother Glen the phone. Their conversation was quite short because the next thing he told me was that she was on her way. We all sat in the waiting room terrified of what we thought Tiana's outcome may be. The next question was, where the hell was Big Dred? No one could reach him or even had a clue as to where he was. I became so angry that this man was nowhere to be found and yet my niece was back there fighting for her life.

I began asking others to try and locate him. Just then, my girl, my bestie Carol rushed over to me to find out what was going on. I couldn't really get into all the gory details because just as I started talking to her, the doctor walked in, looking for me.

"Ms. Jay!" he called.

"I'm here!' I replied.

He asked what my relationship with the patient was and he then asked for her next of kin. I screamed. I knew he was getting ready to tell me the worst. But he calmed me down and told me to please listen and cooperate. He asked me again but this time all I could do was point to Michelle, indicating to her to walk over. As she approached, she asked my mom to come, too and the doctor asked us to follow him into a more private setting to talk to us. When my mom got closer to the doctor, he did a double take and called my mom's name. He wanted to know what she was doing here.

"Yes, Dr. Herlow, it's me. This is my granddaughter," she said.

"Really? By all means, hurry up and follow me," he demanded. Man, was I glad my mom was there! It made the doctor and his staff work even harder to save my niece.

When Dr. Herlow took us inside the chapel, he told us he had to level with us and be straight forward. He told us at this point, he had no idea what was wrong with Tiana and he needed our help. We had to tell him as much information as possible about her as we could. From her allergies to the reason for her being in the ER. I wanted him to save my niece but it seemed that he was more focused and concerned about the well-being and safety of the baby at that point. He wanted us to be aware there was a chance she wouldn't make it, and, at this point, she was on life support. He further explained to us that they would continue to run a series of tests to ascertain more information and he would definitely keep us posted. As I began to walk out of the chapel, I began to break down even more. I sank into the arms of my dear friend Carol whose shoulder was there for me to lean on. I was a wreck, not knowing if my niece was going to live or die was weighing heavily on my heart. The more Carol tried to console me, the worse I got. Nevertheless, I was so grateful that she was there for me. She went to the restroom to get me some tissue, and as soon as I turned around, who walked through the door but Mr. Big Dred himself! Finally he had made it to the hospital. I didn't know how to take him being there but I was determined to keep my cool.

As Carol came back towards me I noticed she and him spoke as they passed each other at the entrance. She immediately came and sat beside me and whispered in my ear.

"Jay, look! You see that dude right there coming in the entrance way?"

"Yeah, I see him, why? What about him?"

"He's handsome, eh, a sexy looking dude, isn't he?"

"Huh, yeah, I guess. Why?"

"You would never know he was sick, would you?" As I looked again to make sure we were looking at the same person she said it again.

"You would never know he was sick, would you?" Which clearly messed me all the way up. I was completely taken by surprise and at a loss of words, so I asked her what she meant by him being sick. She stared at me again, and with the strangest look on her face, she repeated, "He's sick!" I started to hyperventilate, begging her to define the word sick.

By that time, Carol was getting very upset too because she felt like I was playing dumb. But with that strange look on her face, she was inadvertently telling me to read between the lines. I sighed in despair. "No, Carol, no! Do you know who that is?" I asked. She looked over at him and then she glanced back at me and uttered, "Yeah, why? His name is Derric. He was an inmate and my client at the prison. But Jay you can't say anything, I wasn't supposed to tell you."

"Why not?" I asked.

"Bitch, because I'm a sworn officer and I could lose my job."

I dropped to my knees, feeling quite weak holding my face in my hands mumbling,

"Oh, my God! Oh, my God!" Then I yelled, "Oh, my God!" I felt sick to my stomach!

She grabbed me and asked me how I knew him and with tears streaming down my face, I whispered in her ear, "That's Tiana's boyfriend!"

"Oh, no!" Carol replied. I immediately jumped up and ran over to my momma trying to talk to her before he got near the rest of the family but he was coming fast to try and find out why all the whispering and suspicious movements were all about. Carol was trying to calm me down and keep me away from him. I pulled my momma to the side and informed her about the devastating news I had just received. She immediately went to find Dr. Herlow and requested he run one or two more very important tests.

He granted that request and had my mom, Michelle and myself return to the chapel to sit and wait for the results. The wait seemed like forever as we sat and waited on Dr. Herlow's return. I was angry, very angry. My niece was on life support battling and they wouldn't even let us see her. All we could do was wait, and I was praying that the outcome would be better then what we were expecting. I asked Carol not to say anything else to Big Dred. She promised that she would not. I got my other siblings together to let them know that the situation was more or less under control.

And, the thing is, I couldn't go into full details, but they knew very well not to let Big Dred out of their sight. For the next hour we sat there, patiently waiting on Dr. Herlow to give us more details on Tiana's health. Man that was the longest nightmare I've ever had. Just as we got ready to go in search of one of the nurses, there was Dr. Herlow, coming up the hallway. When he walked in the chapel, he wanted to know the direct next of kin before he proceeded with his information. That part ruffled our nerves. And with careful consideration, Michelle told us she loved all of us but she only wanted my mother and myself in there with her to hear the news, whatever it was. So Dr. Herlow excused everyone out of the chapel and sat us in front of him as he began to read the results of Tiana's test. He began calling off things on the list that neither Michelle nor myself could understand; we were looking completely lost and confused at each other. Luckily my mom was there to console and translate. She would nod or say ok, then translate into 'plain English. We found out that her blood sugar was too low, causing her to pass out going into a diabetic coma. But what he said next really caused an emotional breakdown. It seemed that our worst fear had become a reality. Dr. Herlow hesitated and grabbed my mother's hand; you see, the test she had him run on Tiana came back positive, thus, creating this world-wind of symptoms for her body to shut down so quickly."

"What test was that, Jay?" Dr. Maxwell inquired.

"The test was the Human Immunodeficiency Virus, Acquired Immune Deficiency Syndrome. The HIV-AIDS test, Doc, HIV! My niece had contracted HIV! That was our worst nightmare!"

To say we were devastated would have been an understatement. My mom and I tried desperately to comfort Michelle since she had just passed out from the tragic news. I couldn't stop crying, my heart had dropped into the pit of my stomach and I felt as if my world had ended, these words that Dr. Herlow spoke sucked the life right out of me. I couldn't breathe, I was literally weeping like a baby. I couldn't pull myself together at this point because I just knew my niece was going to die. Dr. Herlow grabbed my mother's hand and told her she had to be strong; actually, he comforted all three of us with the same words. But I was not trying to hear that; I really wanted to see my niece.

"Please, Dr. Herlow, I need to see my niece." I begged.

"Calm down, I really need you ladies to calm down. I completely understand your grief right now," he said.

"I know it's no easy news for any family to digest. Take a deep breath; now is not the time," he continued.

He wanted us to realize just how serious this battle was and that we had some very hard decisions to make. There was a point where we had to decide whether we were going to save the baby and let Tiana die, or, save Tiana and let the baby die, or give them both a fighting chance. Both scenarios were equally devastating. As Dr. Herlow gave us the run down as well as the pros and cons of our decisions, we sat there clinging to each other, trying to offer some sort of comfort. Obviously, the decision was going to be a no-brainer. But I guess it was his job to explain so he continued. I needed to see her. And since our decision was easy, or so I thought, Dr. Herlow prepared and prepped us to go in and see her. I really wanted to go into the waiting area and put my hands all over this dude, but I had to see Tiana first.

Dr. Herlow returned and escorted us back to the Intensive Care Unit where Tiana laid. On our way, my brother Glen approached us.

"What's going on?" he asked hesitantly, but at that moment I just couldn't respond. All I could tell him was to be patient and that we were headed to see her now, and it didn't look good at all. I really couldn't explain at that moment; however, I wanted him to know that he was not to let that devious Mr. Derric out of his sight. I tried to catch up with my sister-in-law, my mom, and Dr. Herlow. As we entered Tiana's room, we could not believe our eyes. This was harder than I thought it would be… by far the hardest situation I've endured in my life. Looking at Tiana's lifeless body connected to all those tubes, I.V.s, pumps and a bandage tightly covering her entire head was overwhelming. I couldn't make sense of anything I was seeing. I stood there confused, lost and in a daze. We slowly arched our way towards each other, bowed our heads fervently, and began to pour out our hearts to Almighty God. The air was tense, the atmosphere was somber. We entreated God for a miracle! All stood still. Each time that oxygen was pumped into her body, it gave me hope that something would change.

I prayed that she would start breathing on her own and wake up from this horrible nightmare. Dr. Herlow decided he'd explain to us our options one more time as the time was drawing near. Michelle didn't have a clue of what she should do.

"What! Huh…I don't believe you!" I yelled. I couldn't understand why she didn't know what to do; this was her daughter. I was angry, but I know I couldn't override her decision. I pleaded with her not to give up hope. Constantly trying to make her see why she shouldn't give up hope either. I wasn't taking the news well when I lost my cool, and I told her that if she unplugged my niece she'd better be ready to go, too. Hindsight dictated that to be a cruel and insidious remark, but that was just how I felt. I couldn't accept the fact that she was giving up so fast. Then I turned to my mom, trying to convince her to make Michelle see the blunder she was making. I know Dr. Herlow mentioned the possibility of Tiana being brain dead or in a vegetative state, but I still wasn't about to surrender.

Michelle and I began having a shouting match about the whole situation, but she couldn't take all the yelling I was doing so she had me removed from the room. Apparently, according to them, I was out of control and needed to calm down. My mom then decided to give Michelle sometime alone while she came to talk to me. You see, my mom was displeased with my behavior, and I couldn't get her to understand why we shouldn't give up. All she kept telling me was that I needed to have respect for her wishes because this was such a hard decision for her. The loss of my brother wasn't easy and now losing her daughter was even harder. This hurt me to the core but after listening to my mom and all that she had to say, I kind of understood. But I still refused to let go. She wrapped her arms around me and told me it's all up to God, it's in His hands, and I had to believe, accept and remember that. Well, truth be told, I knew all of that, but, I still wasn't going to capitulate to the will of her mom. I was resolved to be strong and fight for life, not death. Then she advised us to remember the good times we shared and embrace the life she lived and let's go say our goodbyes.

By that time, Dr. Herlow was telling one of the nurses to gather the rest of the family from the waiting area so that they all could say their goodbyes as well. One by one, they brought my brothers, sisters, nieces and nephews back into the room to watch the ventilator work. None of them had a clue of what was going on; all they knew was that Tiana was dying and we had to say goodbye. It was a total shock to them as well. Saddened by all the grief, I stood and watched my family come together. Shattered, torn and brokenhearted, we stood there and watched as the nurses began to disconnect her. But someone was missing. Chase.

"Where's Chase?" I asked my brother. When he informed me that he was still in the waiting area with Derric. I lost it.

"What? Go get him now!" I yelled.

My brother was looking lost but asked me if he needed to bring Derric back here, too. And with fire in my eyes and anger written all over my face, I screamed,

"Hell, no!"

My brother was confused but he knew I meant business. He didn't ask another word and walked out to get Chase. When he returned, he wanted to know what was going on, but I still couldn't say anything. However, I did let him know that we would all meet up at the house for a family meeting as soon as we left the hospital. But, I needed to get Chase to his mom before she took her last breath. As I walked into her room with Chase on my hip, when they were turning the machine off. The air was cold and tense; you could've sliced it! A deafening silence permeated the atmosphere as sorrow was written on everyone's face. It was heartbreaking watching them unhook the connecting wires that were breathing for her, and during this process, an innocent baby boy kept calling his mom.

"Mommy…, Mommy! Mommy!" he wailed.

They were down to the last tube…and I stretched out his tiny arm and he touched her hand and kissed her on the cheek as her breathing shortened. I bent down and gave her one last kiss and whispered in her ear,

"Fight, baby…, Tiana, please fight!"

I looked at the monitor as the numbers dropped rapidly. Dr. Herlow was standing next to the machine waiting to record and call the time of death. The tears flowed copiously and the last thing I got to say before being pulled away was, "I love you." My mom grabbed Chase as I walked away. I was engulfed in anger and overshadowed in hurt and pain. There was nothing that could alleviate my pain. I was headed in the direction of the waiting area where Mr. Derric was sitting. I wanted to kill him; I wanted him dead. I wanted him to experience this same pain he had caused my niece and my family. I couldn't contain myself so I began to walk fast because I knew someone was going to try and stop me.

"If only I could get in arm's reach of this dude," I thought to myself. The only problem was that seeing how well my mother knew her child, she instantly knew what I was up to. I didn't realize it at the time, because I wasn't paying attention but I heard her tell my brother, the security guard and the deputy standing in the hallway with us not to let me go out there. It didn't stop me though, it only caused the anger and resentment to swell inside me, and propelled me to move faster. I made an attempt to enter the double doors to the waiting area, I heard Michelle scream. I spun around and noticed that Dr. Herlow and his team putting everyone out of Tiana's room. I stood in the middle of the hallway not knowing which way to go. I wanted desperately to go into that waiting room but I was trying to figure out what was now going on with Tiana. I wanted a miracle!

"Jay, you ok?" my brother Glen asked.

"No! I'm not." I replied. Yet I still couldn't move out of that spot. As I watched my mom and my sister-in-law hugging each other, crying and praying for God to help, Glen grabbed me by the hand and tried walking me back towards the family, but I still couldn't move.

"Dr. Maxwell, give me a second. This hurts so badly."

"What hurts?"

"Just having to relive this whole ordeal."

"Jay, listen, give yourself some time. Let's take a break. You've got to give yourself more time to heal. Take a deep breath, drink some water, you'll be fine. Need some tissue?"

"Yes, please."

"I tell you what, Jay, let's just call it a day. And schedule you another session when it is convenient for you."

"Call it a day? Why? I don't have money like that."

"Don't worry about it, the next one is on me. But there is just one more question I just have to ask. Why is it bothering you so bad? What did he do to you that has you in such a rage? Clearly there is more to this story that you are willing to share."

I dropped my head and sat still for what seemed like an eternity…. a bit shaken and visibly emotional after recounting that terrible experience. Warm tears cascaded the side of my cheeks.

"Ms. Willis, Jay….hello?" Dr. Maxwell inquired.

Listen, I know you're hiding something, but when you come back I want to hear everything, leaving nothing out; all or nothing. Now just go home, relax, regroup and I'll see you again real soon…."

Acknowledgements

First of all I want to thank God for His many blessings, and for allowing me the chance to save someone's life with my story. I thank Him for showing me that through Him all things are possible as long as you trust, have faith and believe. This journey has truly been a struggle and a test, which has now become my testimony and strengthened my faith. To my mother Lucille, One of my biggest inspirations; thank you for your love, guidance, patience, support, and understanding. You've shown me the true meaning of a mother's unconditional love for their child, and I want you to know your sacrifices were never in vain. Words cannot express how much you mean and how grateful I am to have you as my mom. Thank you for never giving up on me. My grandma Overseer Alberta, Thank you for your teaching and your love for God that set the foundation for our family ties. Without you, there is no me. Thank you for keeping me covered and always praying for me. You are the best grandma a girl could ever ask for, my angel on earth. My daddy James, My first love, thank you for showing me what true love feels like. The love and support you've shown me gives me more of a reason to keep going and never give up on love. Thank you for always having my back and being that shoulder to lean on. To my son Trae'von, My world, my heartbeat, my everything. I thank God daily for His biggest assignment issued to me, becoming a mother (giving me you). You've taught me courage, strength and patience but most of all, unconditional love from a son to his mother. I thank God for the unbreakable bond you and I share. You are truly my biggest blessing and I wouldn't trade you for the world. I love you infinitely. To my sister Cheryl, My biggest cheerleader, thank you for always having my back. Thank you for teaching me the true meaning of friendship, loyalty and trust. Thank you for always being that ear to listen when I needed someone to vent and open up to. You are my Shero, lol. I appreciate all that you have done for me. Not only are you my sister but you're my best friend. You were heaven sent indeed. To my brother Andrae, I don't even know where to begin. Thank you for being the best big brother on this side of heaven. You are truly an inspiration and a motivator. Thank you for the tough love you've given me and always pushing me to go higher, letting me know that no matter what, you will always have my best interest at heart. I also thank you for the hugs, and the drying of my tears after all those hard conversations and harsh reality checks. I now understand and know everything you've tried to teach and show me when it comes to this cruel world and the people in it. Thank you for believing in me when I didn't believe in myself. You're a great teacher. To my brother Nate, Thank you for just being you. You have shown me the true meaning of self-worth. You have inspired me in so many ways that it's hard just to name one or two. But I thank God for the courage and strength that He has blessed you with to conquer the obstacles man set in your way. You are truly an inspiration and a blessing to me. And To my brother Daryl, Thanks for your love and support, and all your advice. Whether it be good or bad I know I can always count on you for a good laugh. Stay strong and keep looking up; it's almost over. Jameshia: My step-daughter and my friend. You've filled a void in my heart that only a daughter's love could give. You have truly become my ride-or-die chick. Thank you for encouraging me to do this. All our ups and downs have been well worth it. Our bond is truly one from God. I thank your father for sharing you with me; you are truly a blessing and an inspiration. You've made me proud. I love you. To my sisters-in-law, AnTonia, Lydia, and Mattie: You ladies have played special roles in my family. You three are the best; I am so blessed to have you all in my life. Thanks for always having my back and being there for me even in my darkest hour, always helping me to bounce back and push forward. I love you my sisters. To my godmother and aunt, Ms. Willieceal: Words cannot express my gratitude towards you. Thanks for everything and teaching me to love myself despite what others may say or think. You are truly one of a kind, lol. And to my aunts, uncles, cousins, nephews and nieces; I want to thank you all from the bottom of my heart and to let you know just how much you guys mean to me. You've shown me the true meaning of family first. I love you all dearly and thank you all for always supporting me. I know we may not always agree but I know the love is sincere. To Mrs. Sheneka Lawrence: My angel on earth, another one of God's blessings to me. Thank you from the bottom of my heart. This has truly been a journey but I know you were sent to me from God. You have been by my side through this process, guiding me in the right direction with your words of encouragement. I will forever be in debt to you. Words cannot describe how grateful I am to you. So I'll just say thank you, thank you, thank you for everything. To my editors, Mrs. Audrie Blake and Ms. Sharlyne Thomas: I Thank you ladies for pushing me, for making me dig deep inside in order to birth something great. You both helped make my words come to life. And last but not least, a special thank you to Jonathan Fernandez for the amazing cover artwork, thank you for seeing my vision and making this cover amazing. Thank you all from the bottom of my heart!